M000078872

Patient A

One of the author's sketches for the play.

Jens Bjørneboe

Amputation

Texts for an Extraordinary Spectacle

translated by

Solrun Hoaas & Esther Greenleaf Mürer

edited by Karl Kvitko

XENOS BOOKS

"Jens Bjørneboe og norsk teater,"
Sørlandsk magasin No. 12, 1996, 17-19.
Copyright © 1996, 2003 by Oddbjørn Johannessen

Address applications for production to:
Teaterförlag Arvid Englind Ab
Box 5124, — 102 43, Stockholm 5, Sweden

Translation of the play *Amputasjonen* / *Amputasjon* was made
possible by a grant from Norwegian Literature Abroad (NORLA)

This Xenos Books publication was made possible by a gift
from the Sonia Raiziss Giop Charitable Foundation

Cover art by Jens Bjørneboe
Cover design by Greg Boyd
Book design by Karl Kvitko

```
         Library of Congress Cataloging-in-Publication Data

Bjørneboe, Jens 1920-1976.
  [Amputasjon. English]
  Amputation : texts for an extraordinary spectacle / Jens
Bjørneboe ; translated by Solrun Hoaas & Esther Greenleaf Mürer.
    p.cm.
  Includes bibliographic references.
  ISBN 1-879378-46-9
  I. Hoaas, Solrun. II. Mürer, Esther Greenleaf III.Title.

PT8950.B528 A7513 2003
839.8'2274--dc21
                                                    2002038005
```

Published by Xenos Books, P.O. Box 52152, Riverside, CA 92517
Tel. 909/ 370-2229. Website: *www.xenosbooks.com*
Printed in the USA by Van Volumes, Three Rivers, MA 01080
www.vanvolumes.com

CONTENTS

* translated by Esther Greenleaf Mürer
** translated by Solrun Hoaas

Illustrations by Jens Bjørneboe

A NOTE ON THE TEXTS

The present volume is devoted to a short, but spectacular play by the Norwegian iconoclast, Jens Bjørneboe. It contains, first, one of his articles on the theater, written shortly before the first version of his play and expressing views pertinent to it. The first version follows; its title is *The Amputation: A One-Act Play for Arena Theater* (the original: *Amputasjonen: manasjespill i én akt*). Bjørneboe let the piece lie for five years, then took it up again when the opportunity arose to work with a Swedish director. His correspondence with the director and some of his notes for revision are included here in the section, "Work on a Second Version." The completed second version follows; its title is simply *Amputation* (the original: *Amputasjon*). It was premiered in Stockholm and performed elsewhere in Scandinavia, then received an enthusiastic English-language production in Canberra, Australia. Materials from that production, including program notes, performance stills and excerpts from a review are appended here to suggest the possibilities for new productions. (English spelling in this section is British, but elsewhere — as in both versions of the play — American.) Finally, critical articles on Bjørneboe, placing the play in the context of the European theater and his other work, are provided for the thoughtful reader. Bibliographic references conclude the volume. The author's sketches are spread throughout. Thus it is hoped that everything has been made available to permit the reader to see, whether in the mind's eye or on the stage, an original, extraordinary and cautionary spectacle.

Karl August Kvitko
Editor, Xenos Books

Amputation

Texts for an Extraordinary Spectacle

THE THEATER TOMORROW

Of course, nobody can tell what the works written for the theater of tomorrow will look like.

Which is really too bad, because tomorrow's plays must be written today. Therefore we have to know, even if it's impossible. That means we ourselves must *decide* what tomorrow's dramatic literature will be.

As writers we have only one mandate: over today we have no authority; to directors, publishers and theater managers we are superfluous — the theater needs boys to sell candy, not authors. But: over *tomorrow* we rule with untrammelled, absolute power. The beggar becomes king at the moment he grasps the scepter with full awareness.

And what shall we decide about the plays of the future and thus about the theater of the future?

*****

Let us first state what tomorrow's drama will *not* be. The dynasty of "Bourgeois Drama" in the line of Hebbel-Ibsen-Strindberg-O'Neill has abdicated. Of course, the family has descendants and exiled heirs, but the house is too old, and naturalistic psychology ascribes to middle-class private life a significance that it can only have today for old ladies. Seeing "the battle of the sexes" (read: *family life*) presented on the stage while the world's statesmen are playing with nuclear weapons puts things so out of proportion that it can *only* produce involuntary comedy. The same applies to erotic theater; it belongs behind the scenes and not on the stage. To an even higher degree it applies to "poetic" or "lyric" drama; that belongs to the comedy of private life, because reality has passed it by. The soul and its agonies, "longing," "loneliness," etc. can no longer in all modesty be taken seriously, any more than preoccupation with individual "morals" or "character" or [Ibsen's] "claim of the ideal." Today these things are only usable on the stage to the degree that they are consciously used as irony, i.e. a *distance-creating* anticlimax to the ever more surrealistic madhouse of a world that we help to populate.

This world definitively turned into a criminal asylum at seven o'clock on the morning of August 6, 1945, at the time when the American war leaders first used atomic weapons. On that morning in one fell swoop practically the whole of world literature became obsolete: *it all became a museum.* At precisely seven a.m. both hands stopped on the clock.

What happened was actually as follows:

A scientist made his entrance on the stage, and from under his white lab coat protruded a long, thick, black tail. It was quite clear, not to be mistaken, and everyone could see that it was genuine: inside the lab coat was a tall, dark man with a real tail. Not as an "image" or "symbol" or metaphor, but quite simply the *Devil* in person. His Majesty himself — straight out of the Middle Ages.

I believe it was precisely at this moment that naturalism went under for good. And while the Great Mushroom still stood in the heavens, all political boundaries and all national cultures evaporated out into the cosmos. Their earthly remains persisted as local museums. World literature became a collection of children's books.

At first hardly anyone understood to what extent the Devil had become flesh and dwelt among us. To be sure, the sight of the tail was creepy, but we hoped for a long time that it would be possible to pretend we didn't see it. Today, almost twenty years later, it's easy to show that we didn't succeed. The long, ugly tail is and will remain utterly unforgettable — and it will take some years before we are fully abreast of the situation. Until then we must get used to the tail, keep a clear head and live in the madhouse with all the balance and cheerfulness we can manage. Hedda Gabler's muzzle-loading pistols and Miss Julie's riding crop belong in the cavalry section of the last century's bourgeois military museum. The themes that were the basis for all bourgeois and naturalistic-psychological drama are hard to take seriously when mentioned in the same breath as the 600,000 old people, women, children and unborn Japanese slain in August 1945. Our domestic sorrows are overshadowed by the problem: *What in the world are we going to do with the Devil?!* — It is no longer a question of "beginning with oneself" or "being oneself," "being in the truth," "realizing oneself" — or the ethical fine points of marriage and God knows what fancy dishes they decked the table with in the century's infancy. The situation has become more acute since that time, and we no longer feel sympathy for or interest in a heroine who hangs her head because she has sexual or social troubles. All that has become the stuff of comedy, and the old heroes have become clowns.

In spite of the Devil the old themes still exist, but in future theatrical pieces they must be seen and treated in a different way from before. And in what way?

One of Bert Brecht's most salient traits is that he fell silent at the sight of the Mushroom and the Tail. And Brecht was a very, very wise dramatist. You can search just as long for the Devil in Brecht's works as in the telephone book and the census rolls. Nor will you find a direct reference to nuclear weapons. Both lay outside Brecht's sphere, and indeed outside his *time*. Brecht's period was the era of the class struggle, and he never goes outside his own thematic province. But the moment the uranium bomb was dropped over Hiroshima, all class differences *ceased*. The bomb had no social consciousness; it was a product of the criminally asocial, and it was asocial. Brecht overlooked it. It isn't found in Marx.

Actually Brecht falls silent after this. He quite certainly understood that the epoch that was inaugurated in 1945 was no longer his own, and that his thinking and writing could not meet the time that was now beginning.

As the years go by nearly all literature becomes *harmless*. The same fate that befell August Strindberg, Henrik Ibsen, Eugene O'Neill and all the rest has hit Brecht even harder: his Marxist stage dialectics have become one of the commercial entertainment industry's greatest drawing cards; in the late capitalist world his plays are always good box-office. Brecht is harmless, because he never says a word that touches on the real problems of our time.

The bourgeois drama illuminated the worries of private life; it became "psychological." The drama of the Brecht period illuminated the troubles of society and the economy; it became "social." Behind Friedrich Hebbel lies another world: Friedrich Schiller's "morality" and "idealism," the "idealism" of French classicism and the moralizing comedy writers, Molière in France and Ludvig Holberg in Scandinavia. Bernard Shaw and Oscar Wilde represent special English transitional forms, actually bourgeois comedies with a certain moralizing element of social criticism. Beside these main lines lie other isolated phenomena: Maurice Maeterlinck, later Luigi Pirandello and other pure and halfway "esoteric" portrayers of the private life's twilight hours.

Common to them all is that none wrote plays intended to be performed with the atomic mushroom as a backdrop, so that the plays they did write *must* remain more or less imprisoned as museum pieces — some pure, simple and lovely, others conventional and covered with dust, plus a third group touching and sweet, in the same way that the first telephones and earliest automatic weapons can touch us today when we go through a museum of technology.

It is no hubris to declare that it's all obsolete; on the contrary, it would be an act of total megalomania to claim that any of these things should have survived what happened in 1945, which has truly transformed our conscious life. It would have taken an absolutely unique miracle to single out dramatic literature as the only thing to survive the explosion with its relevance intact. All other spheres of activity in the humanities have been left dangerously far astern in relation to technological science; capitalism and Marxism are obsolete, the banking system is obsolete, the judicial system is centuries behind the times. Practically everything is in a mummy and museum condition compared to the real questions that have arisen in the last couple of decades.

One of the most pleasant means of escaping from these questions is, of course, to immerse oneself in the ancient classics, in the Elizabethans and in Shakespeare, possibly in Greek tragedy — above all to find confirmation of one's wishful dream of "the eternally human," "the timeless," the belief that "the great questions have always been the same." We are willing to do anything, if it can just help us shut our eyes to the fact that today we are facing not merely new problems, but *problems of an entirely new type.*

The questions that confront us are of a purely philosophical kind. And we won't come through our crisis until we have found a fundamentally new way of thinking. From this new way of thinking must arise a new philosophy.

The *new* in our situation today is that for the first time humanity has met itself in earnest.

In every way, in all circumstances and all over the world it is this that has taken place, scientifically, politically, artistically and philosophically: humanity has met humanity. We have met ourselves in Hiroshima, in the dissolution of the colonial world, in China's revolution; in short, we have met ourselves in an ongoing upheaval of all things. In a way, it is the Man with the Tail who has helped us do it, and it is to him we owe our thanks for the fact that our neighbor has become aware of us.

We have become aware of our own awareness.

And we have become aware of other people's awareness.

Humanity's development from dream to a waking state has taken a long time, but the last phase of that development has happened with shocking speed. And right after the moment of awakening we are confused. But it is still more confusing to see that we have arrogated to ourselves all the power without knowing it. It is the philosophical and intellectual aspects of this whole situation that are of interest today.

Writing for the stage in earlier times — to the degree that we are talking of plays of any significance — by turns illuminated "the religious," "the ethical," "the psychological" and "the social." What now confronts us is the philosophical, the purely intellectual aspects of every situation. The task at hand — note this well — is to *make them visible*.

Undoubtedly this is a more difficult task than any of the previous ones, because it must be carried out so consciously, and because it involves giving flesh and blood to more subtle things than before. The more intellectual the abstraction becomes, and the more abstract the *thought* is, the more dynamic and concrete the representation must be. We can also say: the more spiritual the philosophical content becomes, the more physical the incarnation must be. When it comes to writing for a wholly intellectual theater, we can then be certain that the manuscripts must, to a much higher degree than before, take on the character of a scenario, and the acting style must become more pantomimic and physical than before.

This is the same development that our environment has gone through; the problems are far more abstract than previously, and the consequences are reflected in a correspondingly more physical way. Erroneous thinking can exterminate whole cultures. Similarly, behind the most horrible physical effects humanity has hitherto produced — Hiroshima and Nagasaki — lay the most abstract thinking that has so far been achieved. The most striking thing is thus the degree to which abstract thought has been incarnated in matter.

The same must apply to the theater: the philosophical content will not come to life in dialogues or monologues as before — but must be ever more directly incarnated in physical stage processes.

That is, the thought — in the form of image, metaphor — must become wholly visible. The metaphor must be taken literally, shown directly — so that there arises an intellectual process, made visible in a clear and logical series of images — of physical (_not mental, and not social either!_) situations. A contemporary theater will thus be scientific and philosophical, and circuslike and physical, all at the same time. Everything must become _action_, and there will be a definitive end to the old statuary declamation of "poetic" or "profound" speeches.

Naturally, this action will be one form or another of a physical fight.

To avoid misunderstanding: every legitimate way forward toward a contemporary theater must go through a real understanding of Brecht's epic theater, with its capacity to refine and purify. The development of the Paris "absurd" school and of the young English drama shows what happens when one has overlooked the fact that Brecht means a turning point in the history of dramaturgy: sooner or later one falls back into pre-Brechtian viewpoints and theater practice, and hence very quickly becomes a museum piece oneself. A museum of modern art is also a museum, and the more slogan-like, specialized and one-sided an art is, the faster it ends up in the glass cases.

(Perhaps it is time to clarify the use of the word "museum," which is used not only in a derogatory or disparaging sense. Not just anything is worthy of a permanent place in a good museum, and it's considered an honor for painters and sculptors to end up in museums while they're still alive. So to say that something belongs in a museum is already a recognition of merit and an expression of respect. Personally, I have a great weakness for museums and visit them diligently in every country I visit — not only out of passion for the objects in their collections, but also because I am fond of the quiet, peaceful, unworldly and meditative mood that always reigns in good museums: the quiet whisper of the transitoriness of all things and of eternity. And you can *learn* in museums. Above all, you can learn what you should *not* do; it is of the very greatest value to know what has been done, and what it is unnecessary to do over again. Besides, the really good museums stand for something in the direction of an Ariadne's clew leading backwards in time; it is good to know that you have a place to come *from*. Without museums we would be homeless in foreign cities. The museums are our common, shared portion of humanity and culture, our most central common possession.)

The problem is that art and the life of the mind don't *arise* in museums; there must always be places outside the walls where something new is being born. For literature the library corresponds to the museum, and we would have a miserable world without libraries.

With regard to the theater the concept changes completely; a so-called "museum theater" cannot preserve anything but the theater's earthly remains — props, costumes and photographs, sketches and models of stage sets, etc. — in other words, only the dead body. The theater itself, this most fleeting and perhaps most beloved of all art forms, cannot be preserved in collections in the same way that pictorial art and literature can. At best, single performances can be preserved in a mutilated condition through tape recordings and documentary films. The true *museum enterprise* takes place on the stage, here and now.

And the awful thing about this is that the public, the critics, directors, theater managers and actors are only very rarely aware of it. Every historical play, whether from Paris of the thirties or from Pericles's Athens, must be a museum piece, even if in lucky circumstances it creates a semblance of life on the stage. And the actors and directors are subject to a fate that no other artists could imagine: they must unceasingly pretend that they can "live themselves into the past," and must also fill their consciousness with words and thoughts that in reality have nothing to do with their own existence — except as a remote analogy. Perhaps the worst thing about it is that the critics by and large believe that that's how it ought to be; *only* the museum is allowed to count as art.

Only when the theater flourished did contemporary drama dominate the stage. This applies to all theater history from ancient times until today, and it is due to André Antoine's immortal contribution that modern plays step out of the museum state — and only then do you discover how difficult is to be a free and independent artist in your own time.

The one wave of post-Brechtian literature for the stage has been the English one — and it was due to a meeting between a few enthusiastic and able theater folk and a series of good plays of mixed psychological and social content. They undoubtedly did much to bolster interest in the theater in England and hence the English theater's position inside its own country, but they didn't bring *the theater* one step further, and their performances abroad already seemed like a traveling museum of English contemporary art. People saw or read the plays with admiration, and nodded and said: "Yes, it must not always be so easy to live in England!" The pieces demanded nothing more of the theaters than a solid and traditional naturalism from the pre-Brechtian period. For modern theater they just meant reproduction of texts.

A group of Parisian expatriates writing in French have had an entirely different significance. The "theater of the absurd" has left lasting traces in theater history, and it has shown that the concepts "stage" and "dramatic art" are far wider and far freer than we thought. It is also a far more philosophical and intellectual theater (and therefore also more *physical*) than the contemporary English theater; in short, a universal theater.

The weakness of the "absurd" school lies in its lack of dramaturgical consciousness and its lack of a relation to Brecht. Its whole iconographic technique lies in pulling out a naturalistic "symbolic" detail and magnifying it up into an "absurd" gigantic format. At times the technique becomes annoyingly formulaic, because the school lacks certain elements of a modern theater that it actually could only have obtained from Brecht; among other things it lacks the distance from the private that only a passion for social problems can give. The absurdists have decidedly seen the man with the tail and the whole atomic mushroom, but because they are missing the simple human will to justice, they fail to acquire the moral authority necessary for a play's relevance.

In Strindberg's *Ghost Sonata* the mummy in the cupboard contains all of the "absurd" in one image, and it is from Strindberg that the movement stems. But they have overlooked the central thing in Strindberg, namely his "old-fashioned" quality, his devoutly religious temperament: he believed in God as Brecht believed in Lenin. Both of them believed in justice — here or in the hereafter.

The "theater of the absurd," then, has a small fragment of Strindberg as a point of departure, and is therefore pre-Brechtian in its essence and in its concept of the theater. That is why the plays so often feel just like petty-bourgeois, private, naturalistic episodes: we've seen this before, and there's no new thought in it. Its merits notwithstanding, the "absurdist" movement lacks the central feature of modern theater and of modern art in general: the anti-illusionary, which in Brecht bears the name "Verfremdung" [Alienation], and which is a very special oscillation between illusion and anti-illusion. It has an intense consciousness-raising effect on the viewer, and is a legitimately modern force.

Some of the most important elements in pantomime theater rest on this feature.

Before we go on, however, we shall look at yet another set of phenomena that we can profit from in a negative sense — the wholly technicized media within the mass-entertainment industry: film, radio theater and TV theater. It is obvious that today nearly all artistically obsolete forms are experiencing a kind of renaissance in these channels; and the more technically perfect they become, the stronger their possibilities in a purely imitative direction: their ability to "create" a naturalistic illusion becomes a temptation for almost everybody who has to do with them. The imitation of nature that was beginning to be antiquated in the theater flourished anew and acquired new possibilities with every technical "advance" made by the technicians of radio, film and TV. The movies illustrate this backward development quite clearly: a Charlie Chaplin film from the beginning of the century is stylistically much more modern than an Ingmar Bergman film of today. And in the latest triumphs — wide-screen, color or even three-dimensional film — all artistic considerations are put aside in favor of the demand for "true-to-life" imitation. The illusion will eventually become so strong that all distance can cease completely.

Something similar happens with radio theater. With its sound effects — paper crumpled to sound like a tiger breaking through the jungle, or whistling wind, thundering trains, etc. etc. — along with a pathetic overuse of the actors' voices, it frolics shamelessly with "dramatic" naturalistic effects that even the most old-fashioned stage theater would blush to use.

Exactly the same thing has rapidly taken the upper hand in TV theater, which combines the film's misuse of naturalistic closeups and common illusory tricks with radio theater's sorry resuscitation of all forms of conversation drama.

These technical mass media have acquired their intense reactionary power through one common trait: they lack the last anti-illusionistic corrective that even the naturalistic stage theater has — including the sight of the stage, the orchestra pit, the heads and napes of the onlookers in front of you, the sense of hearing the audience around you, etc. — in short, all the things that have prevented absolute and perfect naturalism from definitively penetrating the living, *true* theater. In film, radio theater and TV theater these last inhibitions fall away, and the technicians have been able to romp freely and realize their *own* ideals of "art" which shall be "lifelike." This has naturally had its destructive effect on the audience, which — even if it doesn't expect humming car wheels, closeups of drowned people, avalanches and catastrophic floods and snowstorms, copulations and closeups of torture scenes — still wants its theater as true to nature and illusionistic as possible.

For the theater, however, these effects of canned entertainment are harmful only so long as the theater folk themselves fail to draw firm lines, but try to imitate the technical media or compete with them in the use of illusory tricks — be it through manuscript, direction, stage setting — and not least the *style of acting*. The right approach must be the diametrically opposite one:

Let film, radio theater and TV theater keep all their junk, their props and tapes and imitation tigers! Let them blow their train whistles and rumble their sheets of tin, film the eyes of the priest in front of the altar and take closeups of people over abysses, complete with burning bridges and screaming brakes. Let the technicians keep all the trash of 19th-century naturalism, and let us rejoice over the clueless but wonderfully useful trash-removing function they perform:

Whatever film, radio and TV theater are doing, we don't have to waste our time with it on the stage!

The absolute opposite of technical simulations of nature, tricks of illusion and attempts at imitation, is pure *pantomime*. Perhaps the mime works more anti-illusionistically than any other stage artist, competing only with the musical acrobat-clown. Both work through direct ridicule of illusory tricks. Mimes such as Marcel Marceau, Jean-Louis Barrault and Samy Molcho have in common that they are all great observers, indeed *great realists*; what makes them so is precisely their irony and their distance — their contempt for illusion and its technical method: naturalism.

The theater's degeneration can almost always be detected in the use of outward things: in the overuse of machines, technology and equipment. Where the *spirit* is lacking, one instinctively tries to divert the public's attention from inner poverty by substituting outward and borrowed finery in direction, trappings and gestures. One offers illusion instead of truth, and as long as this goes down with the public, one firmly believes that spirit can be replaced by dishonesty, and that the deception won't be discovered. In this way it is almost always the conventional and mercantilized theater of illusion that itself prepares the soil for the coming revolutions and reforms — albeit to the very highest degree against its will.

Pantomime needs three things: a human body, an empty stage and an action. In any case, the rest comes under the heading of things money can't buy.

André Antoine, Jacques Copeau and Bertolt Brecht created their epoch-making theater for less money than what is spent today on making an average Norwegian film. It's an old but unshakable truth that it's almost incredible what can be done by simple means. And today — when film, radio theater, TV theater and illusionary theater have relieved the stage of superfluous nonsense — it ought to be more natural than ever to gather wholly around the basic elements in the theater: the physical situation and the intellectual idea.

In the very image of the mime and the clown there is something that yields an unusual power of penetration; the figure's archetypical quality, its resemblance to an ancient image. The mime is *mute*, and the clown's monologue is limited to [the Swiss clown] Grock and Rivel's eloquent cries — "Acrobat oh!" and "A bridge! A bridge!" — possibly accompanied by musical expressions without words. You never miss a more naturalistic text.

In reality we ourselves are mute, and it is our own horrified muteness vis-à-vis the world that the mime and the clown have taken out of our mouths. If the modern dramatist has words of his own to add to this advanced silence, then they must be very, very central. The immense pleasure we can take in the great mime and the great clown consists precisely in the fact that we *escape* hearing words that aren't central enough.

The clown and the mime don't bother us with painfully superficial solutions of a religious or political sort. Their art is just as free of illusion intellectually as it is on stage. And it is chaste enough not to flirt with destruction and decay. By avoiding all tricks of illusion and all imitative naturalism, both have kept their intellectual purity, their spiritual innocence. This places them in the greatest contrast to the great sorry sellout, the spiritual mass bordello, which the rest of the entertainment industry is.

Some of the most important events of European stage life in recent years come from their quarter; the Wroclaw Pantomime Theater — founded and led by Henryk Tomaszewski — aroused the very greatest attention at the theater festivals in Berlin and Paris, and rightly so. The peculiar thing about the pantomime troupe is that it consists not of soloists and their individual acts, but of an ensemble who together act out a pantomime *theater*. Because of its muteness the theater is cut off from the most direct and naturalistic form of communication — the word — and thereby it seems to acquire a kind of open mandate shared by no other form of theater. It is anti-illusionistic from the bottom up, and for that reason necessarily becomes the freest theater of all. Tomaszewski has broken with the classic pantomime form and works with sound, music, props and sets. Only the muteness remains as a guarantee that no naturalism can be used, only the truly basic elements of the theater. It turns out that there are no limits to how far one can go in destroying illusion; the central, straight theater becomes all the more clearly visible. Tomaszewski's own view is this: "The pantomime theater can only deal with *human beings* — as they experience the world and come into conflict with it. But we must describe them through the objects they meet, that is, objectify them completely. The literature of the future must be created wholly from the stage and not from the desk — we can only renew the theater by going back to its basic elements, and distancing ourselves from all those things from which the technical mass media liberate us."

The pantomime theater, in my opinion, will come to acquire the very greatest significance for the *verbal* stage of the future, for tomorrow's *theater*, and for tomorrow's *theatrical writing*.

Within post-Brechtian dramatic literature it is Friedrich Dürrenmatt who has the sharpest intelligence and the deepest knowledge of the stage. His caustic, analytic intellect stands wholly in the service of the humane. As far as I know, he is the only Brecht disciple who has abided by Nietzsche's dictum: "It is a bad pupil who does not become unfaithful to his teacher." This "unfaithfulness" that Nietzsche demands is, however, the true fidelity, far deeper than that which dogmas, "schools" and trends recognize. It means going on alone.

Dürrenmatt characterizes both himself and his drama by an expression that has gradually become well-known: In a time like this no serious person can write anything but comedies.

I think he's right, because today everything that isn't central enough must needs become unintentionally funny when shown on a stage. Ordinary private life and psychology or social mores can only be presented ironically and with distance — and by our taking the comedy freely upon ourselves. That is soberer and better. No one will get away with seriousness anymore.

Thus we already have certain fragments with which we can begin to create the mosaic: tomorrow's stage literature and its theater will contain elements of the absurd theater's dramatic and stage achievements. It will take as an absolute given Brecht's dramaturgy and his *Verfremdung* praxis. It will have definite links to pantomime theater and its reduction of the theater's basic elements; and not least, it will have much in common with the tragic or comic musical clown.

Intellectually and consciously Dürrenmatt is, I believe, the dramatic writer who stands closest to it today.

What we can predict must be a synthesis of the intellectual-philosophical and the plastic-physical: the body as instrument for *logos* — spirit and body as a unity. Borrowing an expression from medicine, one could christen it "the psychosomatic theater" — the high literary circus.

Translated by Esther Greenleaf Mürer

THE AMPUTATION
A One-Act Play for Arena Theater

CHARACTERS

JANITOR

PROF. FORTINBRAS, M.D. — Supreme Court Surgeon, Head of the Surgical Institute for Criminal Justice at the University Clinic in the capital A.

PROF. VIVALDI, M.D. — Anarcho-Surgeon, Head of the Social-Psychological Surgical Institute at the University Clinic in Bologna.

LUCREZIA — Operation nurse.

ADOLF — Porter.

MR. FORGETMENOT — Patient A, trial specimen at the University Clinic.

MISS ADELOIDE — Medical student, later Patient B.

A FEMALE MEDICAL STUDENT

SETTING

The stage is a dissection laboratory and lecture hall for Social-Pathological Anatomy at the University Clinic.

A big sign over the door: "LECTURE HALL 4B, SOC. PATH. ANAT. DISSECTION LABORATORY. SILENCE!"

A sign over another door: "UNIVERSITY POLYCLINIC. RE-FRIGERATED STORAGE. NO ADMITTANCE!"

In the middle of the auditorium — a large rostrum, surrounded by benches for listeners. In the audience sit two male and two female students, one of the latter being Miss Adeloide.

On the rostrum stands a dissection table and a very large "tea table" with bottles, instruments, tampons, glasses, a couple of old-fashioned office lamps with green shades, Bunsen burners, bottles in different colors with curved spouts like restaurant bottles, enormous injection syringes, bedpan, and other utensils. Other props appear as they are fetched or unwrapped. Quite conspicuous are a number of white plastic bags with red crosses on them.

All the props are old-fashioned, enormous, rusty, tarnished or specked with blood etc. The instruments are medieval, suitable for carpentry.

JANITOR on stage. He claps his hands.

JANITOR: Ladies and gentlemen! Silence! Be quiet! Hello! The Social-Pathological Institute of the University Clinic has the great honor of welcoming the outstanding and world-famous anarcho-surgeon, Professor Vivaldi, M.D., head of the Social-Psychological Surgical Institute at... *(The audience becomes dead silent.)*... the Polyclinic Department of the University Clinic in Bologna.

STUDENTS *(applauding and stamping their feet)*: Bravo! Bravo! Bring him on!

JANITOR: The anarcho-surgeon is going to give a lecture with demonstrations... *(Applause and shouts of "Bravo!")*... and... shhh! QUIET! Ladies and gentlemen, quiet!!! And our very own and highly esteemed disciplinary and criminal justice surgeon — Supreme Court Surgeon, Professor Fortinbras, M.D., Head of the university's disciplinary surgical institute... *(New applause and bravos.)*... will give a brief introduction to our honored guest speaker's lecture...

The students applaud wildly and stamp their feet.

JANITOR: The disciplinary surgeon as well as the anarcho-surgeon will work with living demonstration material from the polyclinic's own isolation ward.

STUDENTS: Bravo! Bravo!

JANITOR: I give the floor to Supreme Court Surgeon, Professor Fortinbras, M.D. *(Deep bow.)* Please, Mr. Disciplinary Surgeon! *(Bows again.)* Please, Professor. *(Bows again. Two huge black suitcases are handed to Janitor. Each has a round white area with a big red cross on it.)* Thank you, Professor, thank you, thank you! *(He deposits the suit-cases and bows.)*

FORTINBRAS enters. He is a large old man, clad in black and with an exceptionally solid build. His face has the pallor of age, and he is bald or white-haired. The audience applauds loudly.

FORTINBRAS: Mrrr... Mrrr... Mrrr... Nurse Lucrezia! NURSE LUCREZIA!
NURSE *(from inside)*: Yes, yes, yes! Coming!

Janitor follows after Professor Fortinbras, lugging his enormous load of suitcases, then he dumps them on the rostrum. He bows.

JANITOR: Here you are, Professor, Sir!
FORTINBRAS: Strip from the waist up!
JANITOR: I beg your pardon, Professor?
FORTINBRAS: Yes, yes, that's right! Take off your clothes!
JANITOR *(backing towards the door)*: Excuse me, Professor, but...

NURSE LUCREZIA enters. She is huge and broad-shouldered, with a yellow complexion and dressed in operating scrubs. The janitor tries to get out, but she stops him and salutes the professor.

NURSE LUCREZIA: At your service, Professor!
JANITOR: Pardon me, Nurse.

He tries to pass by her, but she holds him.

FORTINBRAS: Oh, please undress the demonstration patient, Nurse. He won't do it himself.

Nurse Lucrezia lets go of Janitor, goes quickly over to the professor and whispers a few words in his ear.

FORTINBRAS *(to Janitor)*: So you work here... You have no adjustment problems?

JANITOR: No, no, no, no! Absolutely none, professor!

FORTINBRAS *(looking at him with a diagnostic eye)*: Are you quite sure that you are comfortable with your work here? *(Janitor nods eagerly.)* You are never dissatisfied with anything here? *(Janitor shakes his head emphatically.)* And you desire no changes? *(Janitor as before.)* Your marriage is a happy one?

JANITOR: Yes, yes, yes!

FORTINBRAS: Well, that's what *you* say! As you wish!

He turns away from him, but stops a second and turns towards him again, putting his left hand behind Janitor's head and neck, then holding him with a grip like a vise and turning his face up to make him look at him. With the index finger and thumb of his right hand he lifts Janitor's eyelids to stare at his corneas and examine them closely.

FORTINBRAS *(continuing)*: Are you sure you have *never* wanted to do anything irregular?

JANITOR *(terrified)*: No, no! I have never wanted anything deviant. "As everybody knows, the alleged harmful effects of nuclear weapons are grossly exaggerated."

Fortinbras squeezes Janitor harder around his neck and the back of his head, twisting his face farther upward and staring even more closely into his eyes.

FORTINBRAS: Why are you nervous?! *Look me in the eyes!* Are you telling the *truth* now?

JANITOR *(weakly)*: Yes... yes... the absolute truth.

Fortinbras lets him go so suddenly that he almost falls.

FORTINBRAS: Where are the wall charts, my boy? The *wall charts*!

Janitor runs across the bridge, quick as a flash.

JANITOR: I was just going to get them, Professor. *(Exit.)*

FORTINBRAS *(to Nurse Lucrezia)*: Now for the subject of the experiment, where is it now?

NURSE: In refrigerated storage in the polyclinic, right in there. *(Points.)* It was the professor's guest, Professor Vivaldi, M.D., who insisted that even living material should be kept in deep freeze.

FORTINBRAS: He ought to be taken out now, I think, so that he will be awake for the examination here in the auditorium. *(Smiles, nods.)* Right, little nurse? *(Nurse Lucrezia exit. He calls after her.)* Give him a little injection! I'm sure you can find something out there!

Janitor enters with two huge, detailed and rather old-fashioned wall charts.

JANITOR: Here you are, Professor!
FORTINBRAS: Aha!

Together they hang up the wall charts.

Chart A, under an enormous heading "MAN," represents an ordinary muscleman with open belly, guts, sinews, eye sockets, etc.

Chart B, under the heading "MAN — AN INTERNAL COMBUS-TION ENGINE," represents a human-looking car engine.

FORTINBRAS: As you see, ladies and gentlemen, one can immediately find the analogies between *(points)* exhaust pipe and rectum, muffler and bowels, lights and eyes — even *two* of each! Furthermore: cylinders and muscles, battery and brain, carburetor and nervous system, etc. The car engine, however, has *far* greater adaptability than the human being. Disciplinary surgery is founded on the principle that *man in his present form is of faulty construction* — highly subject to subjective patterns of behavior. Now it goes without saying that all social problems can be solved to the extent that we are dealing with non-deviant humanity. This is the basis of both general social surgery as well as my own specialty: criminal justice surgery.

NURSE *(entering)*: Excuse me, Professor, the subject of the experiment seems to be getting restless.

Fortinbras listens with raised eyebrows, gives a meaningful nod and points to an enormous injection syringe lying on the tea table. Continuing his lecture, he explains in pantomime to the nurse what she should do, pointing to the syringe, then to various bottles on the table, suggesting that she take a little here, a little there, and fill the syringe, which must be shaken well before use. He demonstrates in pantomime the act of using the syringe with great force.

FORTINBRAS: Later, in actual practice, criminal justice surgery has proven itself to be indispensable not only for the treatment of the manifestly criminal clientele, but far beyond. Practically any kind of deviant behavior can be treated in this day and age.

Nurse Lucrezia has filled the syringe; she shakes it, squeezes out the air and carries it carefully — with the needle up in the air — out to the polyclinic. A scream of pain is heard.

FORTINBRAS: Criminal justice surgery is also effectively used as a preventive disciplinary surgery in connection with adultery, with the establishment of *law and order*... on privates or petty officers in our armed forces... on school children... on *students*... People who *sleep on their stomach* can be cured... people with warts or regular bad habits... Recently I operated most successfully on a young girl for a particular deviant behavior; she was...

JANITOR *(humbly)*: Excuse me, Professor, but your esteemed colleague is waiting. The anarcho-surgeon is quite indignant and says that... *(Whispers in FORTINBRAS' ear.)*

FORTINBRAS *(raising his eyebrows, smiling and shaking his head)*:   No, no, no, of course not! We shall let him operate immediately!... *(Waves the whole matter away.)* Let Adolf roll in the subject of the experiment, and you can fetch Professor Vivaldi yourself... *(Loudly, to the audience.)* Finally, I should just like to emphasize the immense significance of *my own* brainchild, what is called *disciplinary surgery*, which is a natural extension of criminal justice, and one which not only brought me the rank of general in our armed forces, but also yielded me the exalted military honor which you shall soon see, when Nurse Lucrezia has opened the suitcases...

Nurse Lucrezia enters. Fortinbras points to the suitcases, and she opens them. While he continues talking, she takes the following items out of the suitcases and puts them on him: boots of white shiny rubber, a white shiny operation coat that buttons in the back and has numerous blood splotches, including a pair of obvious hand- and footprints, both blood-red, and finally the Iron Cross with Oak Leaf, which she hangs around his neck. (Applause!) She pours liquid into a washbasin to let him sterilize his hands, after which he holds them up in the air for a long time to let her put black rubber gloves on him, as well as a kind of white officer's cap with gold trim. When she has finished dressing him, she sits on the suitcase and puts on a huge pair of leather ski boots.

While this is happening, ADOLF rolls in an operating table on wheels, equipped with, among other things, the two stirrups of the kind used by gynecologists.

PATIENT A lies motionless under a sheet, completely covered.

Adolf is an athletic type, like a weight lifter or Tarzan, with smooth-shaven, muscular arms. He wears a white nurse's uniform with short pants and short sleeves, adorned with a red cross and medical corps insignia. He presents a scary image of carefree hygiene.

FORTINBRAS: ... that have been done in the field of social surgery. Disciplinary surgery has laid the foundation for all future *organized social structures*, and can, as I have said before, only be compared with the ingenious pioneering work of Koch, Pasteur and Semmelweis in *their* fields... the endocrine glands, ladies and gentlemen! THE ENDO-CRINE GLANDS!!! *(He points to wall chart A.)*

At that moment VIVALDI comes in. Everyone looks at him. Physically he is the exact opposite of Fortinbras: he wears a beret; sports a thin, upward curled moustache and black slicked-back hair; has large pop-eyes; and in his manner appears elegant, smooth and artistic, like a magician or actor. Behind the anarcho-surgeon comes Janitor, carrying Vivaldi's elegant, but also very large and heavy suitcases.

FORTINBRAS *(continuing)*: ... here, ladies and gentlemen, on Chart A, you can see... *(The students, whose attention is caught by Vivaldi's entry, begin to applaud. Fortinbras raises his voice considerably.)* On Chart A you can see the endocrine glands marked in RED INK... *(Looks at his colleague and nods.)* By transplanting these — that is, the endocrine glands — on a little boy, a twelve-year-old... endocrine boy... a boy-gland... by transplanting a gland-boy... I succeeded in... in...

VIVALDI: Don't let yourself he disturbed, dear colleague, by all means... the night train to Bologna doesn't leave until ten o'clock tonight... and it is really such a long time since I have heard a physician mention the endocrine glands that I am delighted to listen... *(Scathingly sarcastic.)* Do continue, dear colleague, do continue!

FORTINBRAS *(furious)*: Allow me the great pleasure of introducing my most learned and distinguished colleague, the world-famous anarcho-surgeon from that immensely worthy institution, the Psycho-Social Surgical Institute at the Social-Pathological Research Center in Bologna: Professor Vivaldi, M.D., who holds the chair in neuro-anatomy at the same institute.

Vivaldi bows; the students applaud and stamp their feet. Shouts of "Bravo!"

VIVALDI: I thank you! I also thank my distinguished colleague for his lecture on the so-called endocrine glands. My own specialty — anarcho-surgery, ladies and gentlemen — is not based on the so-called endocrine glands, on which judicial surgery places such high expectations, but directly on the anatomical structure of the cerebrum; on the incredibly detailed, exact, scientific-empirical charting of the *brain mantle*! And on the most precise observations of the science of general neuro-anatomy. Anarcho-surgery has transformed psychology and psychiatry into scientific disciplines of great precision, ladies and gentlemen: Human consciousness is a neuro-anatomical problem.

FORTINBRAS *(shaking his head, angry and indignant)*: An endocrine problem, doctor! *En-do-crine!!*

VIVALDI: My method is empirical! *(To Janitor.)* There, in the suitcase! *(Sits down on the demonstration object and holds his arms straight out in the air in front of him.)* If the demonstration object is still alive, I shall prove what I have said by using my electroscalpel! *(To the audience.)* One must dare to use bold combinations! Win new territory! New currents! Walk untrodden paths!

FORTINBRAS: Human consciousness is a function of the endocrine glands, and the only hope for law-abiding life lies in effective glandular surgery.

Fortinbras writes on the board: CONSCIOUSNESS = GLANDS.

Janitor begins dressing Vivaldi in his operating coat, red rubber boots and elbow-length red rubber gloves, adding the Legion of Honor, but leaving the beret in place.

VIVALDI *(while being dressed)*: Let us not mince words, dear colleague, but also let us decide the matter by means of objective research through an empirical method! *(To Adolf.)* Would you be so kind as to wake up the demonstration patient, porter? *(To Janitor.)* The instruments, if you please! Thank you, my friend!

FORTINBRAS: Nurse, the instruments, please!

Janitor and Nurse Lucrezia begin unpacking the instruments. Adolf tries to wake up Patient A, who is lying lifeless under the sheet. He doesn't remove the sheet, but only lifts it at the bottom and slaps the patient on the soles of his feet, without result. He rubs the patient's stomach vigorously, lifts his arm and drops it again: it falls down, lifeless.

VIVALDI: It would be a nuisance if the patient had died of his own accord.

FORTINBRAS: No, no, no! It has merely received a slight overdose from the nurse. *(Leans over Patient A.)* The endocrine glands, professor! *The glands!*

VIVALDI: The brain mantle, professor! Transplantations, the recoupling and rearrangement of impulse-channels. *(Reassuring.)* But, of course, together with extensive, primary amputations!

FORTINBRAS: Now you're talking! Amputations are a must!

VIVALDI *(shaking Fortinbras' hand)*: Shall we begin with a cross-examination of the subject of the experiment? While you wake him, I shall say a few words to the auditorium...

The instruments are unwrapped. They are large, heavy, old-fashioned and crude carpenter's tools with patches of blood and rust: knives, tongs, coarse-toothed saws, axes, steel wire, braces, drills, etc., but also iodine, brandy and boric acid, needle and thread and so on.

VIVALDI: Ladies and gentlemen! In my countryman Dante's masterwork, *La Comedia Divina,* you will find a couple of lines, often translated, concerning melancholy, clinical depression, as Dante, fully in line with the authority of the Church, allocates a particular horrendous pool of mire in the Inferno for those human beings who in full sunlight had given themselves over to the vice of melancholy. In the original the lines go like this:

Fitti nel limo dicon: Tristi fummo
Nel aer dolce, che dal sol s'allegra
Portando dentro accidioso fummo:
Or ci attristiam nella belletta negra.

"We were despondent in the mild air that rejoiced in the sun!" ... Today through anarcho-surgery we have fortunately eliminated Dante's problem — that is, by inserting a scalpel into the patient's brain mantle or nervous system, at the anatomically precise spot!

FORTINBRAS *(bent over Patient A, who despite the vigorous massage, does not wake up)*: Now, you *mustn't* ignore the endocrine glands, dear colleague! Here you are! Be my guest!

He passes the gurney with Patient A over to Vivaldi, who sends it back again.

VIVALDI: Neuro-anatomy, Professor! *(Shakes his head.)* I'm afraid you'll have to wake him by chemical means.

Both doctors go back to the tea table, which is now full of bottles and instruments. Fortinbras takes an enormous ampule and fills a huge syringe with it. They inspect it together. Then Vivaldi takes a bottle and pours a little from it into the syringe. Fortinbras shakes the syringe well, pours a little from another bottle and holds the syringe up against the light. They look at it and nod to each other. Fortinbras wants to go over to Patient A, but Vivaldi stops him, points to a third bottle and looks at him questioningly. Fortinbras nods. They pour a bit from this one too, shake the syringe and hold it against the light, look at it and exchange satisfied nods. Applause. They bow. At the patient's side they each offer the other the honor of performing the injection.

FORTINBRAS: After you! — No, you first!
VIVALDI: No, you first!

Fortinbras inserts the hypodermic. It has no effect. They look at the patient for a while, then in surprise at each other. Vivaldi lifts the patient's hand and drops it. It is lifeless. He holds his pocket mirror in front of A's mouth. Fortinbras lifts a leg and drops it, with the same result. They shake their heads. Fortinbras puts his ear to A's chest.

FORTINBRAS: Uh, Nurse Lucrezia, you don't happen to re-member what you gave him... I mean: just approxi-mately?

NURSE: No... I'm afraid I've forgotten. *(Looks at him sharply.)* It was the professor himself who showed me what I should use.

FORTINBRAS *(stroking his forehead)*: Yes, of course. But now it's completely gone... all gone! Isn't that curious, Pro-fessor?

VIVALDI: Yes, it is quite amusing what one can forget while operating! I have a colleague in Milano who forgot his pince-nez on a volvulus in a patient's abdominal cavity... Ha, ha, ha, ha! And no one could figure out why the patient did not recover, ha, ha, ha, ha! But then we X-rayed him... *(Both laugh.)* And then we framed the X-ray, and it still hangs on the wall at the old University Clinic... *(They chuckle.)*

FORTINBRAS: Ha, ha, ha, ha! Well, we all do things like that once in a while. That reminds me of something that happened in Heidelberg some time ago... but I won't tire you with it... Excuse me, Janitor, *you* don't happen to remember what we gave this one, do you? *(He whacks Patient A on the chest. Janitor shakes his head.)* Nurse, have you no idea what he got? *(Gives her the syringe.)* I mean, if perhaps you experimented a bit on your own... just by trial and error? Well, you know what I mean — a little of this and a little of that. You usually have good luck in such things! Just take what you feel like trying, and mix it together... but shake it well!

During the following scene, Nurse Lucrezia, Janitor and Adolf get together at the tea table, where they mix liquids, take turns shaking the syringe, confer and experiment.

VIVALDI *(sitting down on the operating table by the patient):* We can take it easy for a moment. *(Points to Patient A.)* The subject of the experiment will not run away.

Vivaldi lights a cigarette. Fortinbras fetches a bottle and two glasses from the medicine table; he pours them and lights a cigar.

FORTINBRAS: Help yourself! Skol! *(They drink.)* I'm afraid I haven't the least bit of faith in that neuroplastic art of yours... *(Shakes his head.)* Not the least bit...

They drink up. Vivaldi refills the glasses.

VIVALDI: And that patching up the glands *I* consider to be shoemaking, plain and simple. Bah! Skol!
FORTINBRAS: Brain mantle and neuroplastics! Ridiculous!

They drink.

VIVALDI *(hits Patient A):* What was he committed for, anyway?
FORTINBRAS: Social indications... It is seldom anything else. *(Casually, indifferently.)* He is a deviant in practically every respect, in his whole pattern of behavior... *sleeps on*

his tummy... It was the mailman who reported him... He also sits on a bench in the park at night... caught by the police several times...

They drink up.

NURSE: Got it! Here it is. *(She holds the syringe in front of her with the needle up.)* May I?

The professors rise, and Vivaldi chivalrously lifts the sheet to make available the patient's rear end. Nurse Lucrezia takes her place there, and the Janitor and Adolf come closer to watch. Slowly and with great force she drives the needle into the unconscious figure, bends her back and with a great effort, teeth clenched, squeezes the piston up through the cylinder until the liquid is forced into the patient.

Patient A at first lies without moving, then gets up in a "bridge" on his feet and the back of his head; then he shoots into the air with a howl and remains standing on the table with the sheet around his ankles. He is dressed in the striped pajamas of the university clinic — a thin, slight, delicate and frightened little man.

PATIENT A *(moaning)*: Ohhh — What have I done to you!? *(Lifts his arms in fear.)* Leave me alone!
FORTINBRAS: Bravo, Nurse! He's come alive!

The students stamp their feet, clap and shout "Bravo!" Nurse Lucrezia accepts the applause.

FORTINBRAS *(continuing, to A)*: Attention, man! *(To audience.)* Ladies and Gentlemen! Here you can see a clinical prototype, an excellent example of the correlation between case history and constitution! *(To A.)* Stand up straight! Strip from the waist up! *(To audience.)* No doubt you are going to see the usual physique of a deviant: narrow chest, slack stomach muscles, protruding shoulder blades, thin limbs, curved spine, pale and sallow skin and angular hips... *(To A.)* You can take your bottoms off too, and let the audience get a good look at of you. But first get your top off, man! *(Loudly.)* GET UNDRESSED!!

Patient A stares at the instruments. Adolf grabs him to take off his top.

ADOLF: Come here!

But A has seen enough. He jumps over the dissecting table, with Adolf in pursuit. A is quick as a rabbit and runs towards the exit, where one of the students jumps up and stops him, then holds him down on the podium for a second. Patient A squirms free — with the power of mortal dread — and runs through the theater, followed by Janitor and Adolf. He is chased back onto the stage again, but gets under the dissecting table and up among the public benches, where he tries to get back to the polyclinic and the refrigeration room, etc., etc. Finally Adolf gets a hold of him, uses a police grip and twists his arm up between his shoulder blades, forcing him down on his knees with his back bowed.

ADOLF: Now then! Will you be a good boy?
PATIENT A *(with heartrending cries)*: Oh, ohhh! Mommie! Mommie!!
ADOLF: Ya gonna be a good boy now!?
PATIENT A: Oh, Jesus Christ! Oh, God! Yes! Yes!

Adolf loosens his grip, but A has again caught sight of the instruments and breaks away, wild with fear.

[35]

FORTINBRAS *(to Nurse)*: Get him, Nurse Lucrezia. Go get the mouse, Kitty!

She charges after A, who now finds both exits blocked by the students and Adolf. She grabs him once on the floor, but he gets away and crawls between the others' legs. She catches him again on the rostrum and this time uses a "half nelson" on him, then a "full nelson," and finally a "reversed waist-grip." Once she has him down on his back, she rolls him over on his stomach and very roughly bends one of his legs up against his buttock, at the same time thrusting her left foot with the ski boot into the small of his back. He lies pinned as if in a vise, while she smiles at the professors.

PATIENT A: Oh, God! Ohhh... Almighty God! Oh, Jesus!

The students stamp their feet and clap and shout "hurrah!" and "bravo!"

VIVALDI: May I now begin to examine the subject of the experiment?

FORTINBRAS: By all means, professor. But don't let him fool you; he's hiding something. *(To his assistants.)* Put him on the table again, but hold him tight!

They throw him up on the table with his feet over the gynecological stirrups. Adolf holds his feet, Nurse Lucrezia and Janitor — his arms. Patient A lies completely exhausted, as if lifeless. Then he lifts his head, just barely, but lowers it again. Fortinbras looks over towards the tea table.

FORTINBRAS: Are the instruments ready, Nurse?

NURSE *(in a military manner)*: Yes, sir, Mr. Supreme Court Surgeon! Ready!

FORTINBRAS: And the local anaesthetic?

He takes a knife and studies it.

NURSE: All ready, professor! The syringe is loaded and sterilized!

FORTINBRAS: Go ahead, Doctor. You can now give the diagnosis from your own examination.

Fortinbras sharpens the knife thoroughly.

VIVALDI: Thank you. *(To A.)* But you're lying there with your muscles all tightened! Take a few deep breaths and relax. You mustn't get excited, just relax completely now... *(Patient A slowly rises into a "bridge.")* No, no! Now you're getting all tense and strained again! You must smile and feel safe and secure! You are among friends who take care of you and who are fond of you! *(Patient A remains in "bridge" formation. Vivaldi to the audience.)* You see? See that? One can observe a very clear muscular tension, which has produced a kind of carapace or protective muscular armor. *(The students write.)* What is your name?

He rests his body on top of Patient A, who slowly sinks down and lies still.

PATIENT A: Uh... uh... uh...

VIVALDI *(bent over him)*: What is your name?

PATIENT A: Forgetmenot... *(softly)*... Marius.

VIVALDI *(to Janitor)*: Is that his name?

JANITOR: Yes, Professor. His name is Forgetmenot.

VIVALDI: Now listen here, Mr. Forgetmenot. How could you dream of sleeping on your stomach? *(Patient A tries to get loose.)* Did you have a *very* unhappy childhood? *(Loudly.)* Well, *answer me, man!* We have all the proof we need against you. You don't take baths at the fixed times... am I to take it that you really don't *want* to answer?

PATIENT A keeps his mouth shut tight and shakes his head.

VIVALDI *(to the audience)*: One will observe that the subject of the experiment is: a) without reactions, b) emotionally insensitive, c) *incapable of human contact.* But one should never be too hasty in making a diagnosis! Mr. Forgetmenot, you must answer me when I speak to you. *(Loud, brutal and threatening.)* I AM A SOCIAL SURGEON! *(Patient A desperately tries to get loose.)* Mr. Forgetmenot, here is a sugar cube for you! Yum-yum, sugar cube! Mr. Forgetmenot, you have been *observed*! Oh, would you give me the case sheet, colleague? *(Receives it and takes a look in it.)* He has been a traffic nuisance too. Is there anything else, Professor?

FORTINBRAS: I have had it diagnosed a long time ago: *non compos mentis. (Goes to the tea table and fetches the syringe.)* What do you say to a little incision now, colleague? The endocrine gl...

VIVALDI: Not the glands!! *(Indignant.)* Is it you or I who is giving the guest lecture?! I'm just asking. Hand over the syringe! *(Grabs it from him. To the audience.)* With my special technique, it is today possible to attach the lobe of the brain through the nostrils. The muscular armor has its roots in the lobe of the brain.

He sharpens his knife.

FORTINBRAS: The endocrine glands!   *(Grabs hold of the syringe and tries to tear it away from Vivaldi.)*   It's *my* syringe!   *(Tears it away from him.)*

VIVALDI: The lobe of the brain!

FORTINBRAS: The endocrine glands!

VIVALDI *(to the audience)*:   Let us say that — by means of a simple incision — you link the optic nerve to the ears and *vice versa*, the olfactory nerves to the organs of taste, the palatal nerves to the olfactory organ.   The subject of the demonstration will end up *hearing* light and *seeing* tones, *smelling* his food and *tasting* the fragrance of perfume.   If from there you proceed a step further, and link, let us say, *erotica major*, the large sexual nerve, to, for instance, the nerves at the roots of the hair, in the scalp, then the experimental material will experience the most peculiar sensations each time he combs his hair, or if someone strokes his head, for instance.   Here you have the great possibilities of anarcho-surgery in a nutshell!   *(Goes to the tea table and fetches a rough brace for drilling, a weight on a string, a chisel, a hammer, etc.)*   No questions?   Well, then...

The operating lamp is lit.   Vivaldi takes a big knife and a white plastic bucket from the tea table, puts the bucket by the gynecological table and bends over Patient A, who resists with all his might, fighting for his life while Nurse Lucrezia, Janitor and Adolf hold him down.

VIVALDI *(continuing)*:   We once again register a classic deviant symptom: the patient has *no sense of security*. Note that!   *(Nurse Lucrezia, Janitor and Adolf brutally force A to lie motionless.)*   Mr. Forgetmenot!   Would you like to be alone for a bit?   *(Fortinbras approaches with the large syringe.)*   Are you so eager to return to that comfy little isolation cell of yours, Mr. Forgetmenot? *(Vivaldi sharpens his knife.)*

PATIENT A *(shrieking)*: Yes!!

VIVALDI: As you see, a blatant asocial disposition... Would anyone like to ask a question or two before my distinguished colleague now gives the injection?

He nods politely and pleasantly to Fortinbras and lifts the sheet a little while pointing to the belly of the patient.

FEMALE STUDENT: Professor, could it be that he just likes to sleep on his tummy?

VIVALDI: Li... li... li... likes!!

STUDENT: Yes... uh... maybe he doesn't really mean anything... by it... but just likes it... and likes to be alone, I mean... you know, to walk around like that... by himself...

FORTINBRAS: Stand up! *(She stands.) Who are you?*

STUDENT: Uh... uh... A... Adeloide... medical student, born in Winkelsspfuhl... 19 years old... schizoid... appendix removed at age 11... *Community above individual*, Professor! *As everybody knows, the alleged harmful effects of nuclear weapons are grossly exaggerated.*

FORTINBRAS: "L-i-k-e!" You are a student, what do you mean by "like?" Huh?!

ADELOIDE: Uh... uh... I, I meant... nothing maybe... just that, you know...

FORTINBRAS: "You know," "uh," "uh," "you know..." What?! Do you have your dossier and summary with you? Of course, you meant something by... *

Vivaldi points to Patient A and gives signs that he is to be anaesthetized immediately and placed over on the dissecting table.

Fortinbras leans over A, pulls Adolf aside and whispers a few words to him, whereupon Adolf looks at Adeloide and then at the exit, not letting go of her with his eyes. Fortinbras holds Patient A's feet tight with the weight of his own body, then leans over him and with great force pushes the syringe up under the sheet. Patient A strains and stretches with all his might in the most terrible convulsions, screams loudly once and suddenly falls lifeless down on the table. Nurse Lucrezia lifts him by herself over onto the dissecting table, where he lies as if dead. Vivaldi meanwhile has taken over the interrogation of Adeloide.

VIVALDI: Pardon me, little Miss Adeloide, but be quite calm now, little lady... Relax completely and don't worry. Breathe deeply a few times now and don't tighten your muscles... that's it, that's better. And now, just answer my question frankly and openly. Do you yourself sleep on your stomach?

Adeloide, frightened, looks around and then runs for her life towards the exit, which is cut off by Adolf. She turns and runs through the auditorium towards the door of the polyclinic and the cold-storage room. Janitor, Nurse Lucrezia and Adolf carry her squirming over to the table where Patient A is lying.

VIVALDI: Now, Miss Adeloide, strip from the waist up.
ADELOIDE: NO!!

He nods to Nurse Lucrezia, who wrenches the sweater off of her.

VIVALDI: Thank you, Nurse! Now listen here, little Miss Adeloide, has it been a long time that you have felt isolated and alienated among your friends and other students? *(Pause.)* Perhaps you don't like to answer questions? *(Pause. To the audience.)* As you can see, a highly developed syndrome: a) underdeveloped adaptability, b) infantile attitudes of negativism, c) development of Angst, d) emotional coldness, e) lack of contact and f) does not answer questions. We are here faced with a clear picture of poorly developed and permanently impaired mental faculties. Can any of the fellow students and close friends of the subject of the experiment here present complete the profile of social disease by their own observations of further deviations in the subject's pattern of behavior?

FEMALE STUDENT: Maidenhead intact. Sleeps on her stomach.

VIVALDI: Aha!! Marvelous observation! Thank you, thank you! Oh, do undress her below too, Nurse!

A violent, acrobatic fight begins between Nurse Lucrezia and Adeloide, Adeloide resisting with desperate strength and courage. Nevertheless, she is stripped of her clothes item by item until finally she has only her bra and panties on.

VIVALDI *(continuing)*: As you know, anarcho-surgery places *the freedom and dignity of the individual* above all other considerations. *(Leans over Adeloide.)* Have you had problems with your bowel movements in childhood? *(To the audience.)* Many young women are deviants on this important point, take note! *(To Adeloide, threatening)*... and do not stick to the prescribed timetable. Have you had irregular defecation?

ADELOIDE *(in fear of death)*: No, no, no!

STUDENTS: She has been observed!!

Fortinbras comes closer with the syringe.

VIVALDI: Well, then! Show her the syringe, Your Honor, Supreme Court Surgeon! *(To Adeloide.)* What did you mean by saying that the subject of experiment perhaps "just liked to walk around by himself like that?" Do you happen to know what he was *thinking* about when he was walking about like that? What?! — Relax completely now, my dear! We're all so fond of you here... What did you *mean* by that?

ADELOIDE *(broken, weak, lets all hope fly)*: I... felt sorry for him... He was so small and looked so kind... *(Pause.)*

VIVALDI *(extremely gently and kindly)*: Do you still feel sorry for him, my dear?

ADELOIDE: NO!! *As everybody knows, the alleged harmful effects of nuclear weapons are grossly exaggerated.*

VIVALDI *(as before)*: Do you still think he looks kind?

ADELOIDE *(shaking her head frantically)*: No!!

VIVALDI: You may certainly sleep on your stomach, my dear. Turn around, if you like.

ADELOIDE *(in a panic, lifting her head in desperation and trying to get loose)*: No, no, no!!... not on my stomach!!

VIVALDI: Put her on her stomach! *(Janitor, Nurse Lucrezia and Adolf turn Adeloide by twisting her arms and legs. She is still resisting when Vivaldi with great accuracy puts the tip of his finger on her spine.)* Here, Professor! Right in between the eighth and the ninth vertebrae!

Deep, complete silence. Fortinbras raises the syringe while Vivaldi washes the spot in alcohol. Adeloide cries and whimpers. Fortinbras gives the injection, quick and firm; at the same moment Adeloide lets out a piercing scream, short but loud, twists around a little on the table without anyone holding her. Then she lies lifeless, with hands and feet off the edge of the table.

VIVALDI *(resuming)*: Thank you, dear colleague! Thank you... *(He nods to everyone.)* Now it is over. *(Wipes the perspiration from his brow.)* Poor dear... and now she'll feel good, so very, very good! *(Goes to the dissecting table.)* Ladies and gentlemen, we shall now begin the neuro-plastic operation here prepared, basing it on immutable anarcho-surgical principles...

FORTINBRAS *(furious)*: Now, listen here, dear colleague! I protest against such an obvious example of malpractice! Transplantation of endocrine glands is the only method to consider in this case!

VIVALDI: I am the guest lecturer!

FORTINBRAS: I draw to your attention the fact that I am a bearer of the Iron Cross with Oak Leaf. I want so much to operate.

VIVALDI: I draw to *your* attention that I hold the Grand Cross of the Legion of Honor! And I am invited here to carry out the operation!

FORTINBRAS: As the responsible head of The Surgical Institute for Criminal Justice I cannot allow the operation to be carried out... unless...

He looks at Vivaldi and becomes thoughtful.

VIVALDI: ... we could come to an agreement?
FORTINBRAS: Yes.

He sits down and thinks.

VIVALDI: Let's say you take the glands, and I take the brain mantle.
FORTINBRAS *(gets up and gives him his hand)*: It's a deal!
VIVALDI: I stand by my word.

They shake hands like sportsmen.

FORTINBRAS: Oh, Nurse! Bring the slop buckets here! Put them there, that's it. Thank you, thank you! And the instrument table. Thank you, Nurse.

The surgeons choose their instruments, and everything is put in order for an aseptic operation.

FORINBRAS *(continuing)*: Dear colleague, let us begin.

He lifts his knife.

VIVALDI: Ready, get set...GO!

He puts the drill to Patient A's crown, and a moment of silence follows.

VIVALDI *(shouting)*: Say, colleague!
FORTINBRAS: Yes?
VIVALDI: Do you remember in the year 1848 when old Professor Langenbeck carried out that thigh-bone amputation in front of a full auditorium at the old Benevolence Hospital in Berlin... the whole operation, including ligation of blood vessels and veins, with skin, muscle and fascia incisions, as well as sawing off the bones, in 37 seconds flat?! What do you say to that?
FORTINBRAS: Nurse Lucrezia! *(Over the sound of Vivaldi's drill.)* Nurse! The stopwatch is lying on the instrument table.

Nurse Lucrezia finds the stopwatch.

NURSE: Ready, Professor!
FORTINBRAS: My dear colleague, before you open the cranium, I shall take the thigh bone!

[45]

VIVALDI: The bucket, the bucket! *(Something falls into the bucket.)* All right! NOW!!

Both work like mad. We hear only sounds of tools: hammer, drill and saw. Once in a while a splash is heard in the buckets. Adolf runs out with the parts to the deep-freezing room...

VIVALDI: Stop! Finished!

FORTINBRAS: You win, Professor. But you won't begrudge me a rematch, I trust? Will you take the other thigh-bone amputation while I finish off with the glands?

VIVALDI: With great pleasure!

They change places.

VIVALDI *(continuing)*: Nurse, will you give the signal to start?

NURSE: One-two-three, GO!

They work in silence.

FORTINBRAS: The slop bucket, Adolf! Quick! *(Adolf carries it out.)* To the specimen unit.

VIVALDI: The bucket.

Splash again. They sew.

FORTINBRAS *(raising his hands)*: Stop! I'm finished!

VIVALDI *(the same)*: Me too!

NURSE: Supreme Court Surgeon, Professor Fortinbras, M.D. won by one and a half seconds.

Tremendous applause.

[46]

VIVALDI: That business with the glands is veterinary science, pure and simple; it has no therapeutic value.

FORTINBRAS: You're a poor loser, dear colleague.

VIVALDI: The terms were unequal. The glands are child's play. But... what if we now took an arm each, so that we'll have exactly the same task, and start together. Is it a deal?

FORTINBRAS: Of course! Agreed! Give the signal to start, Nurse.

They change places again and take up starting positions.

FORTINBRAS *(continuing)*: Are the slop buckets ready, Adolf?

NURSE: One-two-three, GO!

Just as before, blows, sawing, but also heavy sighs and gasps from the surgeons who are beginning to get tired. Then two splashes are heard almost simultaneously. Adolf carries both buckets out. The surgeons sew with big, swinging arm movements, quickly and for a long while. Adolf returns.

VIVALDI *(lifting his hands)*: Finished!

FORTINBRAS *(same as Vivaldi)*: Finished!

NURSE: Two tenths in favor of the anarcho-surgeon!

FORTINBRAS: Congratulations! *(Applause from the students.)* What is it, Nurse?

NURSE: There seems to be something wrong with the patient; he's not breathing.

She shakes her head in disapproval. Fortinbras puts his ear to A's chest and listens, while Vivaldi accepts his applause. Fortinbras then draws Vivaldi over to A; they both listen, look at each other and shake their heads, shrugging their shoulders.

VIVALDI: Why should he have to breathe?

FORTINBRAS *(spreading a sheet over A)*: Oh well! *(Points to the polyclinic.)* Adolf! The deep freeze! Specimen unit. *(To Nurse Lucrezia.)* And now for Patient B, Nurse. Roll her under the lamp... over here! *(Points. Adeloide is rolled under the lamp. He looks at her, turns to Vivaldi.)* Ah well... Poor little thing! What would you suggest, dear colleague? The glands?

VIVALDI *(pats Adeloide lovingly, gallantly and with obvious flirtation)*: I should have loved to take her along to Bologna... now that spring is here... the spring in the great auditorium on the north side. *(He breathes heavily and turns to the audience.)* "As everybody knows, the alleged harmful effects of nuclear weapons are grossly exaggerated."

He is interrupted by the loud ringing of an electric bell. The students applaud and start to get up.

JANITOR: There will be a forty-five minute break for lunch. Next performance starts at exactly 1:15 p.m.

Students applaud.

— E N D —

Translated by Solrun Hoaas

WORK ON A SECOND VERSION

I. *Correspondence with Swedish Director Martha Vestrin*

10 December 1969

Thank you for your letter which I just received yesterday.

It all sounds good, and I want to write about what you suggest. Actually I once wrote a short piece for arena theater which treats of much the same theme. I only published it in a little magazine, but I will get it out again and see if I can use it as a basis. It's a surrealistic and crazy little piece about mental and physical violence against the "abnormal," i.e against all who have individual inclinations. It takes place during a medical lecture, in *disciplinary surgery*! The piece was written *before* the student revolt and is thus clearly prophetic. It was a joke which turned serious.

I would be very glad to see you here as soon as possible, so that I can get a wholly concrete foundation for the play.

All that you tell about the way of working seems very appealing — but I must also have more concrete ideas of the *style of acting*, so that the play can be tailored precisely for *this* theater.

4 February 1970

... I enclose the scene about Forgetmenot. I hope that you as a trained theater-surgeon can transplant these different limbs and organs, according to how they — surgically seen — fit into the play.

The sequence you propose in your letter seems to me just right — and also it would produce the strongest effect to see Forgetmenot alive just before he is to be operated on.

Do you need more material?

What the hell should the play be called? "The amputation" is merely a working title. Do you have a suggestion for a title? — "Normalization"? "Adaptations"? Can you find some quasi-scientific buzzword which is trendy in Sweden at present, and which also covers the play?

I assume that you have received the three first scenes. And I repeat that you may use them quite freely. Today we're going to the Munch Museum to see Eugenio [Barba] and the Odin Theater. It will be wonderful to meet the old mafioso again.

Four interpolated scenes — all retrospective

Insert 1

The combination nurse and porter "Adolf" is subjected to normalization, in the form of military drill unto insanity, as in the French Foreign Legion, the German SS, the American "cage" or the Marines — in which he is humiliated and crushed totally, until all humanity is stamped out of him. The abasement refers to inter alia "unofficial viewpoints" and to "the cage." Scene acrobatic and brutal unto bestiality. Wash the floor with toothbrush, etc etc. Normalization successful.

Insert 2

Operation nurse Lucrezia is normalized. She is brainwashed until everything personal and individual is gone. The method is both physical and mental. Everything private is washed out of her, to the advantage of "society": she is forced to betray her beloved — her original words and opinions are replaced with phrases learned by heart like "Community before individual," etc., along with slogans from advertising, party politics etc., plus psychological and psychiatric cliches/ stereotypes. Normalization successful.

Insert 3

Patient A, "Forgetmenot," is subjected to *unsuccessful normalization...* He is unusable, militarily, socially and economically. After the treatment he has a relapse, disturbs traffic, sits on a bench, falls in love. He withstands torture and brainwashing, never betrays his beloved or anybody else. Is finally brought in for surgical treatment for the incorrigible — to the state's disciplinary clinic.

Insert 4

Patient B, "Adeloide," has been subjected to normalization with an apparently good result. That is an illusion: she commits betrayal, but is not changed at bottom, she rattles off all the phrases by heart — but without believing in them. She never learns to love the State above all else; and she has a secret love history, which was never consummated, therefore she remains *virgo intacta* and sleeps on her stomach. As a student she goes along with the game, but without a true inner glow. She is observed by her comrades, who are all schooled in betrayal and informing. It is only during today's lecture that she is fully unmasked, and must share Forgetmenot's fate.

II. *Foreword to the first publication of* Amputation *(Oslo: Gyldendals Norsk Forlag, 1970)*

Amputation was begun six or seven years ago, and remained untouched until the fall of 1969. A fragment of the first draft was printed in *Ordet*, but at that time I didn't expect to find a theater with an acting style which would make possible a production acrobatic/physical enough to match the style of the play.

Since then much has changed in the state of the theater, and once the expanded version was finished at the beginning of 1970, the world premiere followed shortly thereafter. I thank the Swedish ensemble for its loyal, humane and professionally helpful collaboration.

The world premiere of the revised version — *Amputation* — took place at the Svenska Riksteatern (Swedish State Touring Theater) in Stockholm on April 1, 1970, directed by Martha Vestin.

III. *Notes for the Oslo production of* Amputation *by the Svenska Riksteatern, directed by Martha Vestin (1971)*

The play builds on a fragment, almost ten years old, which was expanded and completed in the winter of 1970, partly in collaboration with the ensemble and Martha Vestin. Formally and technically the play is utterly different from my other dramatic works; it is made for arena theater, and is a wild, almost surrealistic play — partly sinister, partly comic — and with a decidedly physical style of acting which fully exploits the ensemble's high acrobatic and technical standards.

Here, as in _Semmelweis,_ the attack is directed against those forms of society which do not allow room for people who think differently from those in power; but while in the former play the position of the individual was illuminated through a semi-documentary description of an independent scientist's battle for the truth, here it is the weak — the "research subjects" or "the living preparations" — who represent the deviant (i.e., not "productive" and "positive") view of life. The play takes place in a world of tomorrow which extends the authoritarian features of our present social systems, be they designated as "dictatorships" or "democracies." The action is set in an operating theater in a medical school, where the day's advanced social and disciplinary surgery is being demonstrated. The surgeons are not content with amputating the limbs of the disciplinary patients and research subjects; they also interfere in their spiritual lives by means of brain and gland transplants to fit them for the loyalty which society requires. The piece also gives other examples of "normalization processes" to which this society subjects its disobedient members, by such means as brainwashing under military drill and a systematic devaluing of the human being; and with a mixture of (literally speaking) bloody seriousness and farcical satire it shows how those in power manipulate people's feelings and abilities and make them into tools to serve their own interests.

Translated by Esther Greenleaf Mürer

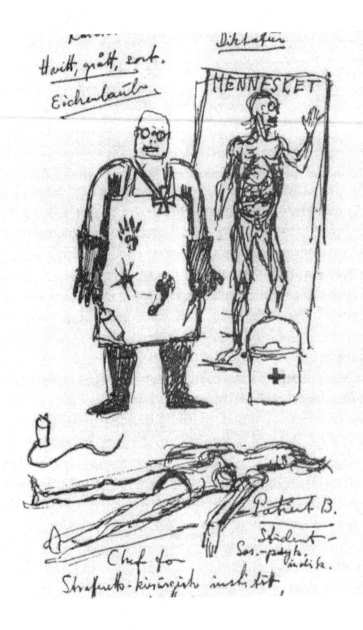

Dr. Fortinbras & Patient B

One of the author's sketches for the play.

AMPUTATION

CAST

PROF. FORTINBRAS, M.D. — Supreme Court Surgeon
PROF. VIVALDI, M.D. — Social Surgeon
LUCREZIA — Operation nurse
ADOLF — Male nurse
MR. FORGETMENOT — Patient A
ADELAIDE — Medical student, Patient B

OTHERS
*(played variously by the six actors
who play the main roles):*

CAPTAIN
SERGEANT I
SERGEANT II
ANDREAS
CHIEF OF POLICE
OFFICER I
OFFICER II
GOTTFRED
DAD
MOM
FEMALE OFFICER

Sounds of the student audience — on tape

Sounds of the amputation — likewise on tape

SETTING

The stage is a lecture hall at the Social-Pathological Anatomical Institute of the University Clinic.

A big sign over the door: "LECTURE HALL 4B, SOC. PATH. ANAT. DISSECTION LABORATORY. SILENCE!"

A sign over another door: "UNIVERSITY POLYCLINIC. RE-FRIGERATED STORAGE. NO ADMITTANCE!"

In the middle of the auditorium — a large rostrum, surrounded by benches for listeners. In the audience sits a medical student, Miss Adelaide.

On the rostrum stands a dissection table and a very large "tea table" with bottles, instruments, tampons, glasses, Bunsen burners, bottles in different colors, thongs, bonesaw, enormous injection syringes, bedpan and other utensils such as are found in a well-equipped, modern operating theater. An operation lamp that can be moved in all directions. Other props as they are fetched or unwrapped. Quite conspicuous are a number of white plastic bags with red crosses on them.

NURSE LUCREZIA on stage. She claps her hands.

NURSE: Ladies and gentlemen! Silence! Be quiet! Hello!
The Social-Pathological Institute of the University Clinic
has the great honor of welcoming the outstanding and
world-famous social surgeon, Professor Vivaldi, M.D., head
of the Social-Psychological Surgical Institute at... *(The
audience becomes dead silent.)*... the Polyclinic Department
of the University Clinic in Minsk.

STUDENTS *(applauding and stamping their feet)*:   Bravo!
Bravo! Bring him on!

NURSE: The social surgeon is going to give a lecture with demonstrations... *(Applause and shouts of "Bravo!")*... and...
shhh! QUIET! Ladies and gentlemen, quiet!!! And our
very own and highly esteemed disciplinary and criminal
justice surgeon — Supreme Court Surgeon, Professor
Fortinbras, M.D. ... *(New applause and bravos.)*... will give
a brief introduction to our honored guest speaker's
lecture...

STUDENTS: Bravo! Bravo!

NURSE: The disciplinary surgeon as well as the social surgeon
will work with living material from the polyclinic's own
isolation ward...

The students applaud wildly and stamp their feet.

NURSE: I give the floor to Supreme Court Surgeon, Prof.
Fortinbras, M.D. *(Low curtsy.)* Please, Mr. Disciplinary
Surgeon! *(Curtsies again. ADOLF throws out two huge
black suitcases to her. Each has a round white area with a
big red cross on it.)* Thank you, Professor, thank you very
much.

FORTINBRAS enters. The audience applauds loudly. Smiling and bowing, he receives the applause in stride, as a celebrated actor.

FORTINBRAS: Mrrr...   Mrrr...   Mrrr...   Nurse   Lucrezia!
    NURSE LUCREZIA!
NURSE: Yes, yes, yes! Here I am. Adolf!

ADOLF enters, picks up the suitcases and lugs the enormous load forward. He bows.

ADOLF: Here you are, Professor, Sir!
FORTINBRAS: Strip from the waist up!
ADOLF: I beg your pardon, Professor?
FORTINBRAS: Yes, yes, that's right! Take off your clothes!
ADOLF *(backing toward the door)*: Excuse me, Professor, but...

Adolf tries to leave, but Nurse Lucrezia stops him. She salutes the professor.

NURSE: Yes sir, Professor!
ADOLF: Pardon me, Nurse.

He tries to pass by her, but she holds him in a judo grip.

FORTINBRAS: Oh, please undress the demonstration-patient, Nurse. He won't do it himself.

Nurse Lucrezia lets go of Adolf, goes quickly over to the professor and whispers a few words in his ear.

FORTINBRAS: So, you are a male nurse here... Well, well, well! You have no adjustment problems?
ADOLF: No, no, no, no! Absolutely none, Professor!

FORTINBRAS *(looking at him with a diagnostic eye)*: Are you quite sure you are satisfied with your work here? *(Adolf nods eagerly, frightened.)* You are never dissatisfied with anything here? *(Adolf shakes his head emphatically.)* And you desire no changes? *(Adolf as before.)* Your marriage is a happy one?

ADOLF: Yes, yes, yes!

FORTINBRAS: Well, that's what *you* say! All right.

He turns away from him, but stops a second and turns towards him again, putting his left hand behind Adolf's head and neck, then holding him with a grip like a vise and turning his face up to make him look at him. With the index finger and thumb of his right hand he lifts Adolf's eyelids to stare at his corneas and examine them closely.

FORTINBRAS *(continuing)*: Are you sure you have never wanted to do anything irregular?

ADOLF *(terrified)*: Yes, yes! I have never wanted anything deviant. "Community above individual!" — "As everybody knows, the alleged harmful effects of nuclear weapons are grossly exaggerated."

Fortinbras squeezes Adolf harder around his neck and the back of his head, twisting his face farther upward and staring even more closely into his eyes.

FORTINBRAS: Why are you nervous?! *Look me in the eyes!* Are you telling the *truth* now?

ADOLF *(weakly)*: Yes... yes... the absolute truth. I have been normalized!

Fortinbras lets him go so suddenly that he almost falls.

[59]

FORTINBRAS: Aha, so you are normalized — well, what do you know! And the normalization brought the desired result?

ADOLF: One-hundred percent. It says so here on my tag.

He hands the professor the tag that he wears around his neck.

SCENE A

VOICE: This is the way that Adolf was normalized.

The light changes.   Adolf is alone with CAPTAIN and SERGEANTS I & II.

CAPTAIN: Is that so? You have your own opinion?
ADOLF: No, I only thought that...
CAPTAIN: Thought that...? Thought?!
ADOLF: I believed...
CAPTAIN: Captain!
ADOLF: Captain! I believed, Captain, that...
CAPTAIN: Believed! Thought!
ADOLF: I just thought that it wasn't necessary to...
CAPTAIN: Captain! Repeat it ten times, and loudly!
ADOLF: Captain!
CAPTAIN: Louder! Before we're through with you we'll
    have you crawling up the walls! Louder! And ten times!

Captain and Sergeants form a circle around him.

ADOLF *(screaming)*: Captain!
CAPTAIN: Louder!
ADOLF *(with all his might)*: Captain! *(Repeats ten times.)*
CAPTAIN *(suddenly hitting him in the belly)*: Say, "Thank
    you, Captain."
ADOLF *(bent over double, gasping for air)*: Ohh, God!
CAPTAIN *(to Sergeants)*: Hear it for yourselves, men. He's
    ungrateful. Straighten him up!

[61]

SERGEANT I *(lifting Adolf's head by the hair)*: Say thank you to the Captain!

Adolf can't talk clearly, but stands up almost straight and mumbles some words.

CAPTAIN: Here we are sacrificing our valuable time to teach you common sense, and you refuse even to thank us? *(Hits him in the face. Adolf totters from one to the other — each one hits him in turn.)* Stop! Are you going to say thank you now?

ADOLF: Thank you very much, Captain!

CAPTAIN: And a thank-you-very-much to your superiors. Bow to them!

ADOLF *(bowing)*: Thank you very much, Sergeant!

SERGEANT *(kicks him flat)*: Louder!

ADOLF *(with all his might)*: Thank you, Sergeant!

BOTH SERGEANTS *(kicking him)*: Louder! Louder!

ADOLF *(screaming at each kick)*: Thank you, Sergeant! Thank you! Thank you!

CAPTAIN: Stop! *(Silence.)* Get up! *(Adolf gets to his feet, weak and wobbly.)* Attennn-shun!

ADOLF: Yes, sir, Captain!

CAPTAIN: Louder!

ADOLF: Yes, sir, Captain!

CAPTAIN: Hands on your hips. *(Adolf obeys.)* Knee bends!

ADOLF: Yes sir, Captain! *(Starts to do knee bends.)*

CAPTAIN: Faster!

ADOLF *(continues with increased tempo, soon falls over)*: Ow, ow, ohhh!

SERGEANT I *(kicking him)*: Keep at it, mama's boy!

SERGEANT II *(kicking)*: Get up, prick!

Adolf gets up halfway, on all fours, then on his knees. Gasps for air.

CAPTAIN: We'll continue our morning exercises! This is the radio exercise program for our senior citizens. Lay on your stomach, you filthy prick! Quick!

ADOLF *(getting down)*: Yes sir, Captain!

CAPTAIN: On to pushups! One-two, one-two, and *(rising tempo)* a-one-and-a-two and...

SERGEANT II *(singing as in a radio's morning exercise program)*: One-two, one-two...

Adolf loses his breath, falls in a heap.

SERGEANT I: You're just a hunk of meat!

CAPTAIN: A hunk of *rotten* meat!

SERGEANT II: Be a good boy now?

ADOLF *(almost gets up)*: Thank you, Captain! *(Gasps for air.)*

CAPTAIN: Say that you're nothing!

ADOLF: I'm nothing.

SERGEANT I: Say you're a shit!

ADOLF: I'm a shit!

SERGEANT I: A *stinking* shit. *(Hits him.)*

ADOLF: I'm a stinking shit!

SERGEANT I *(hitting him again)*: Sergeant!

ADOLF *(salutes)*: I'm a stinking shit, Sergeant!

SERGEANT II: Say you're a dirty little ass-fucking fag! Loud and clear!

ADOLF *(shouting)*: I'm a dirty little ass-fucking fag! Sergeant!

CAPTAIN: Say you're a nothing, an idiot, a pig who doesn't deserve to live!

ADOLF: I'm a nothing, an idiot, a pig who doesn't deserve to live! Captain.

CAPTAIN: Ten times! I'm an idiot!

ADOLF *(screaming)*: I'm an idiot! *(Repeats ten times.)*

CAPTAIN: Attention! *(Adolf obeys.)* Teach him the catechism, Sergeant!

SERGEANT I: Community above individual! Loudly! Ten times!

ADOLF *(shrieking)*: Community above individual! *(Repeats ten times.)*

SERGEANT I: I'm a nothing — the state is everything! Loudly! Ten times.

ADOLF *(as before)*: I'm a nothing — the state is everything! *(Repeats ten times.)*

CAPTAIN: Stop! Ten knee-bends! Quick!

ADOLF *(barely managing)*: Oh, oh, ohhh!

CAPTAIN: Ass-fucker! Attenn-chun!

ADOLF *(straightening up)*: Thank you, Captain!

CAPTAIN *(goes slowly around him and observes him closely, with a tiger's eye)*: Community—?

ADOLF: Community above individual, Captain!

CAPTAIN: Well, now. After our little morning exercise we shall retrace our steps and start from the beginning... You said you meant and thought and felt... You said you thought that it wasn't necessary to..?

ADOLF *(shouting with all his might)*: Community above individual!

CAPTAIN: You can relax completely now, my boy. *(Pats him on the shoulder. — Adolf draws back a little, afraid of the hand.)* Speak up. Say what you think. Good boy! Nice boy! *(Pats him again.)* Remember that we are your friends.

ADOLF: I wanted to say that I didn't think you needed to knock the prisoner out cold.

CAPTAIN: Well, well, well! How about that! *(The Sergeants laugh uproariously.)* You know the prisoner from before?

ADOLF: Yes sir, Captain.

CAPTAIN: You're friends?

ADOLF: Yes sir, Captain.

CAPTAIN: Well, well, well! *(The Sergeants roar with laughter.)* You know he broke his oath of obedience?

ADOLF: Yes, but...

CAPTAIN: But? *(Adolf snaps to attention.)* But?!! *(Captain walks slowly round him.)* And a friend means more than your country and the oath of obedience?

ADOLF: You didn't have to hit him like that, Captain!

CAPTAIN: Ah, ah, ah! Listen to our little faggot! He's a humanist, the filthy prick. *(The Sergeants laugh.)* You know what's right? *Answer!*

ADOLF *(now in better physical condition)*: It wasn't right to hit him like that, Captain.

CAPTAIN: Say he deserved it.

ADOLF: No.

CAPTAIN: Give him his gun. *(A Sergeant brings Adolf his gun.)* Hold it above your head, arms straight. *(Adolf obeys; the three watch him a while. Captain to Sergeant II:)* Be my guest! *(Sergeant II hits Adolf in the diaphragm.)* Thank you. *(Adolf is lying on the floor, bent double in pain.)* Lift him up! *(The sergeants get him on his feet again.)*

ADOLF *(gasps)*: God, let me go! Don't hit me any more!

CAPTAIN: Say he deserved it!

ADOLF: No.

CAPTAIN: The gun! *(Adolf lifts it above his head.)* Run in place! *(He runs.)* You shit! Get your knees up! Higher!

[65]

ADOLF *(obeys, but gasps for air)*: Ohh!

CAPTAIN: Faster! Faster! Knees higher! — Sergeant, the catechism!

SERGEANT II: We are born for the state, we live for the state, we die for the state.

CAPTAIN: Repeat!

ADOLF *(running as before)*: We are born for the state, we live for the state, we die for the state.

SERGEANT I: Ten times!

Adolf repeats the statement ten times.

SERGEANT II: What is our first duty?

ADOLF: Obedience, Sergeant.

SERGEANT I: What is our last duty?

ADOLF: Obedience, Sergeant.

CAPTAIN: Stop. You sickening, slimy carcass! Say that you're a sickening, slimy carcass, and can never get enough of a beating.

ADOLF: I'm a sickening, slimy carcass, and I can never get enough of a beating.

CAPTAIN: I'm not human. Anything lower than a corporal is not human.

ADOLF: I'm not human. Anything lower than a corporal is not human.

CAPTAIN: Hold him properly.

They twist his arms and legs.

ADOLF: Ow! Owwww! Let me go.

CAPTAIN: Harder!

They use more force.

ADOLF *(screams with all his might)*:   Community above individual!

CAPTAIN: Say that your friend got what he deserved!

ADOLF: Yes! Oh God! Help me! He got what he deserved. *(He groans.)*

CAPTAIN: Stop! *(The Sergeants let go. Adolf lies almost immobile on the floor.)* Get up and say you're a slimy pig who doesn't deserve to live.

ADOLF: I'm a slimy pig who doesn't deserve to live.

CAPTAIN: Get down on your knees and thank us for trying to make a human being out of you.

ADOLF *(kneels)*: Thank you for trying to make a human being out of me.

CAPTAIN: Tomorrow you will beat the shit out of the prisoner.

ADOLF: Me... Me... No!

CAPTAIN: Hold him!

The Sergeant holds Adolf and forces his head back while the captain beats him. After a blow in the belly and a kick in the crotch, Adolf falls and remains lying on the floor without moving.

SERGEANT I: That did him in.

SERGEANT II: That's just what that slimy carcass deserved. *(Kicks him. Both Sergeants kick him.)* Now he's coming to again.

ADOLF *(half-conscious, makes a feeble movement)*: Community above individual.

SERGEANT: Say you love us.

ADOLF:: I love you.

SERGEANT I: Shall we hit you more?

ADOLF: If you wish, Sergeant. Hit me and kick me. I deserve it.

SERGEANT II: Our boots are dirty.

CAPTAIN: Yes, they're dirty.

SERGEANT: Adolf, come and lick our boots clean!

ADOLF *(hesitates)*: I love you...

CAPTAIN: The boots, Adolf, *the boots!*

ADOLF *(crawls forward and licks the officers' boots)*: Community above individual.

CAPTAIN: Good boy. Very good.

ADOLF: Thank you, Captain! From the bottom of my heart!

He continues to lick the boots.

SERGEANT I: Lick faster!

Adolf obeys.

CAPTAIN: Tomorrow you will whip the prisoner!

ADOLF: Yes, Captain! *(Continues licking.)*

SERGEANT II: Shout that you're a glob of spit!

ADOLF: I'm a glob of spit! Tomorrow I will whip the prisoner. *(Continues licking.)*

CAPTAIN *(to the audience)*: Interesting phenomenon! Humiliation produces hate; hate is powerless against the one who is stronger and has humiliated him, — therefore the hate is intensified and now directed towards the one who is weaker. In this way, hate, systematically engendered, can be utilized in the service of the state.

ADOLF: Community above individual!

CAPTAIN: Well, then, thank us, buddy!

ADOLF: Thank you very much for letting me lick the gentlemen's boots! For the state we are born, for the state we live, for the state we die.

CAPTAIN: Are you ready to beat the prisoner to death tomorrow?

ADOLF: Yes, Captain! Ready! Thank you so much. I'll kill him! Kill him! Kill! *(Continues licking.)*

CAPTAIN: Good, my boy. Tomorrow you may kill him. *(Smiling to the audience.)* All you do is take a man and degrade him in every way. Interesting: when one loses respect for oneself, one loses respect for humanity altogether. Of course, the job on Adolf took much longer, but the normalization was one-hundred percent successful, and today Adolf is totally adjusted to our society.

ADOLF: I am an idiot, a zero, a glob of spit, a nothing... *Community above individual!*

*****

[Return to the lecture.]

FORTINBRAS: So, you are normalized. *(Lets him go quickly, gives him back his collar and tag.)* Where are the wall charts, my boy? The wall charts!

ADOLF *(gets going, quick as a flash)*: I was just going to get them, Professor. *(Exit.)*

FORTINBRAS *(to Nurse Lucrezia)*: Now for the subject of the experiment, where is it now?

NURSE: In refrigerated storage in the polyclinic, right in there. *(Points.)* It was the professor's guest, Professor Vivaldi, M.D., who insisted that even living material should be kept in deep freeze.

FORTINBRAS: He ought to be taken out now, I think, so that he will be awake for the examination in front of the observers. *(Smiles, nods.)* Right, little nurse? *(Nurse Lucrezia exit. He calls after her.)* Give him a little injection! I'm sure you can find something out there!

Adolf enters with two huge, rather old-fashioned wall charts.

ADOLF: Here you are, Professor!
FORTINBRAS: Aha! That's it!

Together they hang up the wall charts.

Chart A, under an enormous heading "MAN," represents an ordinary muscleman with open belly, guts, sinews, eye sockets, etc.

Chart B, under the heading "MAN — AN INTERNAL COMBUS-TION ENGINE," represents a human-looking car engine.

FORTINBRAS: As you see, ladies and gentlemen, one can immediately find the analogies between *(points with a staff)* exhaust pipe and rectum, muffler and bowels, lights and eyes — even *two* of each! Furthermore: cylinders and muscles, battery and brain, carburetor and spinal cord, wires and nervous system, etc. The car engine, however, has far greater *adaptability* than the human being, and the internal combustion engine has *no deviant opinions* whatsoever. Disciplinary surgery — or, if you wish, criminal justice surgery — is founded on the principle that man in his present form is of faulty construction — highly subject to subjective patterns of behavior. Now it goes without saying that all social problems can be solved *only* to the extent that we are dealing with non-deviant human beings.

This is the basis of both general social surgery as well as my own specialty: psycho- or disciplinary surgery.

NURSE *(entering)*: Excuse me, Professor, the subject of the experiment seems to be getting restless.

Fortinbras listens with raised eyebrows, gives a meaningful nod and points to an enormous injection syringe lying on the tea table. Continuing his lecture, he explains in pantomime to the nurse what she should do, pointing to the syringe, then to various bottles on the table, suggesting that she take a little here, a little there, and fill the syringe, which must be shaken well before use. He demonstrates in pantomime the act of using the syringe with great force.

FORTINBRAS: Later, in actual practice, criminal justice surgery has proven itself to be indispensable not only for the treatment of the manifestly criminal clientele, but far beyond. Practically any kind of deviant behavior can be treated in this day and age.

Nurse Lucrezia has filled the syringe; she shakes it, squeezes out the air and carries it carefully — with the needle up in the air — out to the polyclinic. A loud, wailing scream of pain, piercing and penetrating, is heard.

FORTINBRAS: Criminal justice surgery is also effectively used as a preventive disciplinary surgery in connection with adultery, with the establishment of law and order... on privates or petty officers in our armed forces... on school children... on students... People who sleep on the stomach can be cured... people with warts or regular bad habits... Recently I operated most successfully on a young girl for a particular deviant behavior; she was...

NURSE *(humbly)*: Excuse me, Professor, but your esteemed
   colleague is waiting. The social surgeon is quite indignant
   and says that... *(Whispers in Fortinbras' ear.)*

FORTINBRAS *(raising his eyebrows, smiling and shaking his
   head)*: No, no, no, of course not! We shall let him
   operate immediately!... *(Waves the whole matter away like
   a fly.)* Let Adolf roll in the subject of the experiment, and
   you can fetch Professor Vivaldi yourself... *(Loudly, to the
   audience.)* Finally, I should just like to emphasize the
   immense significance of my own brainchild, what is called
   disciplinary surgery, which is a natural extension of
   criminal justice surgery. It is an invention which can only
   be compared with the work of Pasteur, and one which not
   only brought me the rank of general in our armed forces,
   but also yielded me the Nobel Peace Prize!

He bows. Applause.

*Nurse Lucrezia enters. Fortinbras points to the suitcases, and she
opens them. While he continues talking, she takes the following
items out of the suitcases and puts them on him: boots of white
shiny rubber and a white shiny operation coat that buttons in the
back and has numerous blood splotches, including an obvious hand
print and footprint, both blood-red. She pours liquid into a
washbasin to let him sterilize his hands, after which he holds them
up in the air for a long time to let her put rubber gloves on him,
as well as a kind of white butcher's cap with gold trim. When she
has finished dressing him, she sits on the suitcase and puts on a
huge pair of leather ski boots.*

SCENE B

VOICE: This is how Nurse Lucrezia was normalized.

LUCREZIA *(pulling on her boots and tying the laces)*: It's funny to think that I myself have been an enemy of the people once. It was my boyfriend, Andreas, who led me astray and got me to place the individual need before the needs of the state and people. And I actually had a criminal like that as a lover! The most alarming part was that we mixed sex and politics. When we slept together, we could say terrible things about the people and our country. It was as if these blasphemies made both excitement and pleasure more intense than usual. For example, in the middle of foreplay, Andreas might say that the majority is always of low intelligence and that the people therefore are never right. Or even in the middle of intercourse he might say that the government always acts in a criminal manner, or that only the minority could possibly know the truth, and I could answer, just at the moment of orgasm, that the people are nothing, the individual is everything. We felt ourselves intermingle with our orgasm; it heightened the pleasure. In this way, by saying and thinking the opposite of all we had been taught, it was as if we became the only people in the whole world. We became completely dependent on each other too. And even a single wrong or forbidden thought made us both tremendously excited. When we were together, we forgot the whole world. We could do the craziest things. We shouted and screamed and laughed — and we shouted our blasphemies louder and louder. It was like a witches' sabbath, and when Andreas penetrated me, while he mocked the state and fatherland, I thought I was fornicating with the devil himself. That's how marvelous it was! There were no limits to what we could shout to each other, and we often got so wild that we forgot all about the neighbors who could hear the terrible words we said. But there were those who heard us.

ANDREAS *(enters, taking her in his arms)*: Individual above community!

The sexual explicitness of the scene increases as it goes on.

LUCREZIA: To hell with the community!
ANDREAS: To hell with society!
LUCREZIA: To hell with the whole country!
ANDREAS: The people don't exist — only the individual!
LUCREZIA: Freedom is better than force!

Both are getting more and more excited.

ANDREAS: I shit on my country!
LUCREZIA: I shit on the government!

They roar with laughter.

ANDREAS: To hell with production!
LUCREZIA: To hell with the Youth Front!
ANDREAS: I shit on the disciplinary police!
LUCREZIA: The police should be gassed.
ANDREAS: The politicians exterminated!
LUCREZIA: The Prime Minister fried!
ANDREAS: I don't give a damn about the people!

LUCREZIA *(wild with excitement, beginning to tear off her clothes)*: To hell with the people — I only want you!

ANDREAS: It's only he who stands alone that counts!

LUCREZIA *(in complete ecstasy)*: I want to be lazy and disobedient and pursue the good of the individual over the good of the community, and I shall above all else detest the state and my country all the days of my life, and I shall never serve and never obey the state, my country or the people or my superiors all the days of my life... Oh, come, Andreas, come! Come! Quick!

ANDREAS *(pulls off his briefs)*: And I shall sleep on my stomach and fuck in forbidden positions...

They both climb up on the operating table and prepare for intercourse in an unusual position. They laugh with joy.

THE SEX POLICE enter, shouting "Pigs!"

CHIEF OF POLICE: Pigs! We heard everything you said! Every single word about sleeping on your stomach and hating your country.

OFFICER I: We have impartial witnesses to it. Your neighbors...

CHIEF: You've mocked all that is holy: production and the disciplinary police...

OFFICER II: ... and the Youth Front and people and...

ANDREAS *(pulls his briefs back on)*: Goddam fucking filthy informers!

CHIEF: Hit him!

OFFICER II *(knocking him down)*: Pig! You're going straight to a disciplinary camp.

OFFICER I *(kicking him)*: Goddam enemy of the people! We'll teach you what society is, you bloody individualist!

[75]

CHIEF *(to Lucrezia)*: And you'll be sentenced for sexual egotism. After that, we'll have to see if we can make a proper citizen out of you.

Lucrezia alone again.

LUCREZIA: Then began the course that led to my salvation and normalization. But it took me a long time to realize my guilt. I was incredibly asocial and hardened, an orgasmic egotist. I was abnormal to the depths of my soul, degenerate, destroyed — a real enemy of the people. Only the toughest treatment could help. But I really deserved it. How fair and right the punishment was is something I only realized afterwards, when my thinking had changed within me. I deserved every blow, every kick. And above all, it was so right to humiliate me as much as possible: it made me a loyal and obedient servant of the government and the people. I understood my duty and learnt to feel grateful towards the government and the police. The healthiest and best treatment of all was probably the many weeks I spent in a dark cell in solitary confinement. I sometimes would scream for days on end. At times I didn't know who I was. Once in a while they would fetch me out for interrogation, and then back to the dark cell again. Finally I thought of nothing but what they said to me during the interrogations, and gradually I came to understand what terrible crimes I had committed. Alone in the darkness I understood that the punishment was fair and well-deserved.

Re-enter the Sex Police.

CHIEF OF POLICE: What is your supreme desire? You've learned it in school.

LUCREZIA: My supreme desire is to be hard-working and obedient, and to submit myself to the law of community above individual. And I shall love the government and my country above all else, more than father and mother, husband or child...

CHIEF: Stop!

LUCREZIA: ... more than sister and brother, friend and...

CHIEF: Stop!

LUCREZIA *(continuing automatically)*: ... to serve and obey the government and my country in all and everything...

CHIEF *(grabbing her by the hair and bending her head backwards)*: Stop it!

LUCREZIA *(like a record)*: ... for the government and my country and the people are three separate things, but still one and the same...

OFFICER I *(kicks her down)*: Shut up!

She lies silent on the floor.

CHIEF: You know your catechism, but you don't live according to it. It's just empty words.

OFFICER II: We haven't even started your treatment yet. In a few days you'll wish you never were born.

They tie her hands behind her back.

CHIEF: Tell us everything you know about your fiancé and your parents.

LUCREZIA: I don't know anything.

CHIEF: Shall we take your panties off too?

LUCREZIA: No, no! Be good to me... I haven't done anything to you...

CHIEF:: Get her up! *(The Officers get her up on her knees.)* Tell us! Everything you know!

LUCREZIA: They're hard-working and obedient. They haven't done anything.

CHIEF: And what have they *thought?* The thoughts are the most important thing.

LUCREZIA: I don't know.

CHIEF: You'd rather return to solitary then?

LUCREZIA: *No! No!*

CHIEF: Now listen here, my little one, you're on our side then?

LUCREZIA: Yes, Mr. Chief of Police, I'm entirely on your side.

CHIEF: And your bowel movements are regular — at the fixed hours?

LUCREZIA: Oh, yes!

CHIEF: You have no deviation? Never walk around all by yourself? Never unhappy or sad?

LUCREZIA: Never, Mr. Chief of Police.

CHIEF *(strikes her across the face, holds his hand up to her)*: Kiss it!

LUCREZIA *(kisses his hand)*: I'm completely healthy and normal, Mr. Chief of Police.

CHIEF: Is that so? Is it healthy and normal for you not to want to tell us the truth? *(To Officer II.)* Hit her! *(He strikes her across the face.)* Good! *(To Lucrezia.)* Kiss his hand! *(She does.)*

OFFICER II: She's not one of ours.

LUCREZIA: Yes, I am one of yours. With all my heart and all my soul.

OFFICER II: You can become one of us — now.

LUCREZIA: I want to.

CHIEF: You know that we are the strongest, and those who oppose us are weak. And you want to be on the side of the strongest, don't you?

LUCREZIA: Yes, yes! I do!

OFFICER I: Then you must prove yourself worthy. You must choose.

OFFICER II: You must pay what it costs to become one of us.

LUCREZIA: Anything! Do what you want with me — hit me, kick me, I want to be one of you.

OFFICER I: Your will is in my pocket. We decide.

CHIEF: Do you love us?

Lucrezia tries with her hands tied behind her to get her panties off.

LUCREZIA: Yes, I love you, all three of you, the whole people... see! Just come to me!

Roars of laughter from the men.

CHIEF: Do you love *the State?*

LUCREZIA: You are the State. Do whatever you want with me.

CHIEF: The price for becoming one of ours — one of the strongest who have the power — is for you to tell us what you know about your parents and your fiancé.

LUCREZIA *(realizing she has been trapped)*: Oh God!

CHIEF: There is no other way. Otherwise we shall unfortunately have to report that you have been found unadaptable and incurably asocial. It breaks my heart, my dear. You know the consequences...

LUCREZIA *(sinks down)*: Oh, Mama! Ohhh!

[79]

She cries. The three wait silently.

CHIEF: Well then?

LUCREZIA *(to the audience)*: I'll tell you about it. They un-
tied my hands and allowed me to sit down. They were so
friendly. I told them that my father had criticized the
government and the social police, that my fiancé had said
he hated the police, the army and the government. As I
was telling them this, I understood what an asocial environment I had been brought up in. I had tried to pro-
tect these enemies of the people! Gradually I felt great joy
in confessing. I admitted everything, all my innermost
thoughts and desires.

It gave me a feeling of security to confess. I felt as if
I belonged in society again. I was no longer alone.

And I also told them everything I knew about other
people; about my father, relatives and friends. Mainly I
told them about Andreas, how he had seduced me into
mocking and ridiculing our country and our morality, and
about how diabolically wicked he had been when he
taught me sexual egotism. It gave me an even greater
feeling of security to tell everything about him. But I still
wasn't normalized. I still wasn't 100%. One day the
Chief of Police asked if it was true that I had intended to
become a nurse, and if I knew what the Disciplinary
Clinic was. I answered yes in both cases. At the same
time I was terribly scared, because I knew perfectly well
what the Disciplinary Clinic was. I also knew that the
Clinic needed live material, live organs and live subjects
for experiments and transplantations and demonstrations.
And I knew that the organs are kept in whole organisms,
alive but deep-frozen. They get the living material from
among the enemies of the people, and they are used in
social surgery and in disciplinary surgery. In this way

those who have not been normalized can be of use to both government and people. The enemies of the people can be preserved as live material for years, stored in the freezer. From there the path leads directly to the operating table. But the Disciplinary Clinic also needs assistant personnel, as theater nurses during disciplinary surgical incisions. This is where I had to decide and make a decision for life: Either be put in cold storage as live material and supply kidneys, eyes, muscles, limbs and entrails to science, or to serve the government as a disciplinary nurse and a free woman. I had an entirely free choice. No one influenced me. They treated me much better than I deserved. And I understood that the police wanted what was best for me. I understood that the government loved me. I chose to become a disciplinary nurse, and as long as I live I will prove that I'm worthy of the confidence the government has shown in me. I'll show that I'm worthy of my great task: to serve the people and disciplinary surgery.

OFFICER I: This is how nurse Lucrezia was adapted to society. This is a case of a one-hundred percent successful normalization.

*****

[Return to the lecture.]

ADOLF rolls in an operating table on wheels, equipped with, among other things, the two stirrups of the kind used by gynecologists.

PATIENT A, MR. FORGETMENOT, lies motionless under a sheet, completely covered.

[81]

FORTINBRAS: ... among those discoveries that have been done in the field of social surgery. Disciplinary surgery has laid the foundation for all future organized social structures, and can, as I have said before, only be compared with the ingenious pioneering work of Koch, Pasteur and Semmelweis in *their* fields... the endocrine glands, ladies and gentlemen! THE ENDOCRINE GLANDS!!! *(He points to wall chart A.)*

At that moment VIVALDI comes in. Everyone looks at him. Physically he is the exact opposite of Fortinbras. Behind the social surgeon comes Adolf, carrying his elegant, but also very large and heavy suitcases.

FORTINBRAS *(continuing)*: ... here, ladies and gentlemen, on Chart A, you can see... *(The students, whose attention is caught by Vivaldi's entry, begin to applaud. Fortinbras raises his voice considerably.)* On Chart A you can see the endocrine glands marked in red ink... *(Looks at his colleague and nods irritably.)* By transplanting these — that is, the endocrine glands — on a little boy, a twelve-year-old... endocrine boy... a boy-gland... by transplanting a gland-boy... I succeeded in endocrinating... by endocrinating I succeeded in disciplining...

VIVALDI: Don't let yourself he disturbed, dear colleague, by all means... the night flight to Minsk doesn't leave until ten o'clock tonight... and it is really such a long time since I have heard a physician mention the endocrine glands that I am delighted to listen... *(Scathingly sarcastic.)* Do continue, dear colleague, do continue!

FORTINBRAS *(furious)*: Allow me the great pleasure of introducing my most learned and distinguished colleague, the world-famous social surgeon from that immensely worthy institution, the Surgical Institute for Criminal Justice at the

Social-Pathological Research Center in Minsk: Professor
Vivaldi, M.D., who holds the chair in neuro-anatomy at
the same institute and is a recipient of the Pentagon Peace
Prize.

*Vivaldi bows; the students applaud and stamp their feet. Shouts
of "Bravo!"*

VIVALDI: I thank you! I also thank my distinguished colleague for his lecture on the so-called endocrine glands.
My own specialty — social surgery, ladies and gentlemen
— is not based on the so-called endocrine glands, which
are highly overrated by supreme court surgery and which
I shall pass over without further mention, but directly on
the anatomical structure of the cerebrum; on the incredibly detailed, exact, scientific-empirical charting of the
brain mantle, as well as on the most precise observations
of the science of general neuro-anatomy. Social surgery
has transformed psychology and psychiatry into concrete
scientific disciplines of great precision, ladies and
gentlemen: Psychology is a *neuro-anatomical* problem.

FORTINBRAS *(shaking his head, angry and indignant)*: An
endocrine problem, doctor! *En-do-crine!!*

VIVALDI: My method is empirical! *(To Adolf.)* There, in the
suitcase! *(Sits down on the dissecting table and holds his
arms straight out in the air in front of him.)* If the demonstration object is still alive, I shall prove what I have said
by using my electroscalpel! *(To the audience.)* One must
dare to use bold combinations! Win new territory! New
currents! Climb every mountain!

FORTINBRAS: Psychology is a function of the endocrine
glands, and the only hope for law life lies in effective
glandular surgery. *(Writes on the board: "CONSCIOUS-
NESS = GLANDS.")*

VIVALDI *(while Adolf dresses him in his operating coat, red rubber boots and elbow-length red rubber gloves)*: Let us not mince words, dear colleague. But let us decide the matter by means of objective research on an empirical basis! *(To Adolf.)* Would you be so kind as to wake up the demonstration material? *(To Nurse Lucrezia.)* The instruments, if you please! Thank you, my dear!

FORTINBRAS: Nurse, the instruments, please!

Lucrezia begins unpacking the instruments. Adolf tries to wake up Patient A, who is lying lifeless under the sheet. He doesn't remove the sheet, but only lifts it at the bottom and slaps the patient on the soles of his feet, without result. He rubs the patient's stomach vigorously, lifts his arm and drops it again: it falls down, lifeless. Etc., etc.

VIVALDI: It would be a nuisance if the experimental organism had died of his own accord.

FORTINBRAS: No, no, no! It has merely received a slight overdose from the nurse. *(Leans over Patient A.)* The endocrine glands, professor! *The glands!*

VIVALDI: The brain mantle, professor! Transplantations, the recoupling of impulse-channels. *(Reassuring.)* But, of course, coupled with extensive, primary amputations!

FORTINBRAS: Now you're talking! Amputations are a must!

VIVALDI *(shaking Fortinbras' hand)*: Shall we begin with a cross-examination of the material?

FORTINBRAS *(bent over Patient A, who despite the vigorous massage, does not wake up)*: Now, you mustn't ignore the endocrine glands, dear colleague! Here you are! Be my guest! He's all yours.

[84]

He passes the gurney with Patient A over to VIVALDI, who sends it back again.

VIVALDI: Neuro-anatomy, Professor! *(Shakes his head.)* It appears that we shall have to wake him by chemical means.

Both doctors go back to the tea table, which is now full of bottles and instruments. Fortinbras takes an enormous ampule and fills a huge syringe with it. They watch the process together. Then Vivaldi takes a bottle and pours a little from it into the syringe. Fortinbras shakes the syringe well, pours a little from another bottle and holds the syringe up against the light. They look at it and nod to each other. Fortinbras wants to go over to Patient A, but Vivaldi stops him, points to a third bottle and looks at him questioningly. Fortinbras nods. They pour a bit from this one too, shake the syringe and hold it against the light, look at it and exchange satisfied nods. Applause. They bow. At the patient's side they each offer the other the honor of performing the injection.

FORTINBRAS: After you! — No, you first!
VIVALDI: No, you first!

Fortinbras inserts the hypodermic. It has no effect. They look at the patient for a while, then in surprise at each other. Vivaldi lifts the patient's hand and drops it. It is lifeless. He holds his pocket mirror in front of A's mouth. Fortinbras lifts a leg and drops it, with the same result. They shake their heads. Fortinbras puts his ear to A's chest.

FORTINBRAS: Uh, Nurse Lucrezia, you don't happen to re-member what you gave him... I mean: just approxi-mately?

NURSE: Haven't the slightest idea now. *(Looks at him sharply.)* It was the professor himself who indicated what I should take.

FORTINBRAS *(stroking his forehead)*: Yes, of course. But now it's completely gone... all gone! Isn't that curious, Professor?

VIVALDI: Yes, it is quite amusing what one can forget while operating! I have a colleague in Bologna who forgot his pince-nez on a volvulus in a patient's abdominal cavity... Ha, ha, ha, ha! And no one could figure out why the patient did not recover, ha, ha, ha, ha! But then we X-rayed the volvulus... *(Both laugh heartily.)* It was a pair of gold-rimmed glasses, and my colleague had missed them terribly... *(They laugh again until they gasp for air.)* And the X-ray was put under glass and framed, and is hanging on the wall at the old University Clinic... *(They laugh again.)*

FORTINBRAS: Ha, ha! Well, we all do things like that once in a while. That reminds me of something that happened in Heidelberg some time ago... but I won't tire you with it... Excuse me, Adolf, you don't happen to remember what we gave this one, do you? *(He whacks Patient A on the chest. Adolf shakes his head.)* Nurse, have you no idea what he got? *(Gives her the syringe.)* I mean, if perhaps you experimented a bit on your own... just by trial and error? Well, you know what I mean — a little of this and a little of that. You usually have good luck in such things. Just take what you feel like trying, and mix it together... *but shake properly!*

During the following scene, Nurse Lucrezia and Adolf get together at the tea table. Taking great delight and pleasure in their job, they smell and taste liquids, mix them and shake them one at a time, deliberate and talk and laugh while they experiment.

VIVALDI *(sitting down on the operating table)*: We can take it easy for a moment. *(Points to Patient A.)* The material will not run away.

Vivaldi lights a cigarette. Fortinbras fetches a large white bottle and two glasses from the medicine table; he pours them and lights a cigar.

FORTINBRAS: Help yourself! Skol! *(They drink; he refills the glasses.)* I'm afraid I haven't the least bit of faith in that neuroplastic art of yours... *(Shakes his head and fills the glasses again.)* Not the least bit... No, no, not even a drop.

They drink up. Vivaldi refills the glasses.

VIVALDI: And that messing around in the glands — this gland-grabbing of yours — I consider to be shoemaking, plain and simple. Bah! Skol!

FORTINBRAS: Brain mantle and neuroplastics! Ridiculous!

They drink.

VIVALDI *(hits Patient A on the stomach with his flat hand)*: What was he committed for, anyway?

FORTINBRAS: Social indications... It is seldom anything else. *(Casually, indifferently.)* He is a deviant in practically every respect, in his whole pattern of behavior... sleeps on his tummy... It was the mailman who reported him... He also sits on a bench in the park at night... caught by the police several times...

They drink up.

NURSE: Got it! Here it is. *(She holds the syringe in front of her with the needle up.)* May I?

The professors rise, and Vivaldi chivalrously lifts the sheet to make available the patient's rear end. Nurse Lucrezia takes her place there, and Adolf comes closer to watch. Slowly and with great force she drives the needle into the unconscious figure, bends her back and with a great effort squeezes the piston up through the cylinder until the liquid is forced into the patient.

Patient A at first lies still, then he gets up in a "bridge" on his feet and the back of his head; he turns over and stands on his toes and forehead with his bottom up; then he shoots into the air with a howl and remains standing on the table with the sheet around his ankles. He is dressed in the striped pajamas of the university clinic.

PATIENT A *(moaning)*: Ohhh — What have I done to you!? *(Lifts his arms in fear.)* Leave me alone!
FORTINBRAS: Bravo, Nurse! He's come alive!

The students stamp their feet, clap and shout "Bravo!" Nurse Lucrezia accepts the applause.

FORTINBRAS *(continuing, to A)*: Attention, man! *(To audience.)* Ladies and Gentlemen! Here you can see a clinical prototype, an excellent example of the correlation between case history and constitution! *(To A.)* Stand up straight! Strip from the waist up! *(To audience.)* No doubt you are going to see the usual physique of a deviant: narrow chest, slack stomach muscles, protruding shoulder blades, thin limbs, curved spine, pale and sallow skin, and angular hips... *(To A.)* You can take your bottoms off too, and let the audience get a good look at of you. But first get your top off, man! *(Loudly.) Take it off!*

Patient A stares at the instruments. Adolf grabs him to take off his top.

ADOLF: Come here!

But A has seen enough. He jumps over the dissecting table, with Adolf in pursuit. A long, wild chase takes place. A is quick as a rabbit and runs towards the exit, where he is stopped by a student who holds him tight for a second. Patient A squirms free — with the power of mortal dread — and runs through the theater and over the rostrum, followed by Adolf. He is chased back onto the stage again, but gets under the dissecting table and up among the public benches, where he tries to get back to the refrigeration room, etc., etc. Finally Adolf gets a hold of him, uses a judo grip and twists his arm up between his shoulder blades, forcing him down on his knees with his back bowed.

ADOLF: Now then! Gonna be a good boy?
PATIENT A *(with heartrending cries)*: Oh, ohhh! Mommie!
   Mommie!!
ADOLF: Ya gonna be a good boy now!?
PATIENT A: Oh, Jesus Christ! Oh, God! Yes!

Adolf loosens his grip, but A has again caught sight of the instruments and breaks away, wild with fear.

FORTINBRAS *(to Patient A)*: You mustn't be afraid of the
   instruments; you'll get an anaesthetic before we begin the
   experiments, and from then on you won't feel a thing...
   not a thing. *(To Nurse Lucrezia.)* Get him, Nurse
   Lucrezia. Go get the mouse, Kitty!

[89]

*She charges after A, who now finds both exits blocked by the
students and Adolf. She grabs him once on the floor, but he gets
away and crawls between the legs of the professors, up on the
gurney and operating table, under the tables and out on the floor.
Suddenly he stands still and goes toward her of his own accord, his
hand outstretched.*

PATIENT A: Mommie!

*She takes his hand and throws him down with a judo — or karate
— movement. They wrestle on the floor; first she uses a "half
nelson" on him, then a "full nelson," and finally a "reversed waist
grip" — or a similar judo grip. Once she has him down on his
back, she rolls him over on his stomach and very roughly bends
one of his legs up against his buttock, at the same time thrusting
her left foot with the ski boot into the small of his back. He lies
pinned as if in a vise, while she smiles at the professors.*

PATIENT A: Oh, God! Ohhh... Christ! Oh, Jesus!

*The students stamp their feet and clap and shout "hurrah!" and
"bravo!" Nurse Lucrezia waves to them with her free hand, like
an Olympic champion.*

VIVALDI: May I now begin to examine the subject of the
    experiment?
FORTINBRAS: By all means, professor. But don't let him
    fool you; he's sly, and he's hiding something. *(To his
    assistants.)* Put him on the table again, but hold him tight!

*They throw him up on the table with his feet over the gyneco-
logical stirrups. Adolf holds his feet, Nurse Lucrezia — his arms,
both with judo grips. Patient A lies completely exhausted, as if*

lifeless. Then he lifts his head, just barely, but lowers it again. Fortinbras looks over towards the tea table.

FORTINBRAS: Are the instruments ready, Nurse?

NURSE *(in a military manner)*: Yes, sir, Mr. Supreme Court Surgeon! Everything is ready!

FORTINBRAS: And the local anaesthetic?

He takes a knife and studies it.

NURSE: All ready, professor! The syringe is loaded and sterilized!

FORTINBRAS: Go ahead, Doctor. You can now give the diagnosis from your own examination.

Fortinbras sharpens the knife on a leather strap.

VIVALDI: Thank you. *(To A.)* But you are lying there with your muscles all tightened! Take a few deep breaths and relax. You mustn't get excited, just relax completely now... the dissection will not hurt at all. *(Patient A slowly rises into a "bridge.")* No, no, no, no! Now you are getting all tense and strained again! You must smile and feel safe and secure! You are among friends who take care of you and who are fond of you! *(Patient A remains in "bridge" formation. Vivaldi to the audience.)* You see? See that? One can observe a very clear muscular tension, which has produced a kind of carapace or protective muscular armor. *(The students write.)* What is your name?

He rests his body on top of Patient A, who slowly sinks down and lies still.

PATIENT A: Uh... uh... uh...

VIVALDI *(bent over him)*: What is your name?

PATIENT A: Forgetmenot... *(softly)...* Marius.

VIVALDI *(to Nurse Lucrezia)*: Is that his name?

NURSE: Yes, professor. His name is Forgetmenot, Marius Forgetmenot.

VIVALDI: Now listen here, Mr. Forgetmenot. How could you dream of sleeping on your stomach? *(Patient A tries in mortal dread to get loose.)* Did you have a very unhappy childhood? *(Loudly.) Well, answer me, man!* We have all the proof we need against you. You don't take baths at the fixed times... am I to take it that you really don't *want* to answer?

PATIENT A keeps his mouth shut tight and shakes his head, but then lets out a loud and quivering moan of fear.

PATIENT A: Ah... a... a...

VIVALDI *(to the audience)*: One will observe that the subject of the experiment totally lacks a sense of security; he is: a) without reactions, b) emotionally insensitive, c) incapable of human contacts. But one should never be too hasty in making a diagnosis! Mr. Forgetmenot, you must answer me when I speak to you. *(Loud, brutal and threatening.) I am a social surgeon! (Patient A desperately tries to get loose.)* Mr. Forgetmenot, here is a sugar cube for you! *(He turns and picks up a sugar cube with a pair of pincers, holds it up to A's mouth.)* Yum-yum, sugar cube! *(Patient A keeps his mouth shut tight and turns his face away. Vivaldi eats the sugar cube himself.)* Mr. Forgetmenot, you have been observed! Oh, would you give me the case sheet, colleague? *(Receives it and takes a look in it.)* Ai, ai, ai! Didn't I know it?! He has been a traffic nuisance too. Is there anything else, Professor?

FORTINBRAS: I have had it diagnosed a long time ago: *non compos mentis. (Goes to the tea table and fetches the syringe.)* What do you say to a little incision now, colleague? *(Patient A wriggles wildly.)* The endocrine gl...

VIVALDI: Not the glands!! *(Indignant.)* Is it you or I who is giving the guest lecture?! I'm just asking. Hand over the syringe! *(Grabs it from him. To the audience.)* With my special technique, it is today possible to attach the lobe of the brain through the nostrils. You shall see it in a minute! *(Patient A again tries to free himself, mad with fear.)* The muscular armor has its roots in the lobe of the brain.

He sharpens his knife. Patient A struggles violently.

FORTINBRAS: The endocrine glands! *(Grabs hold of the syringe and tries to tear it away from Vivaldi.)* It's *my* syringe! *(Tears it away from him.)*

VIVALDI: The lobe of the brain!

FORTINBRAS: The glands!

VIVALDI *(to the audience)*: Let us say that — by means of a simple incision — you link the optic nerve to the ears and *vice versa*, the olfactory nerves to the organs of taste, the palatal nerves to the olfactory organ. The subject of the demonstration will end up hearing light and seeing tones, smelling his food and tasting the fragrance of perfume. It is, in short, the doctrine of specific sense attributes put into practice. If from there you proceed a step further, and link, let us say, *erotica major*, the large sexual nerve, to, for instance, the nerves at the roots of the hair, in the scalp, then the experimental material will experience the most peculiar sensations each time he combs his hair, or if someone strokes his head, for instance. Here you have the great possibilities of social surgery in a nutshell! *(Goes to the tea table and fetches instruments.)* No questions? Well, then...

The operating lamp is lit. Vivaldi takes a big knife, a bone saw and a white plastic bucket from the tea table, puts the bucket by the gynecological table and bends over Patient A, who resists with all his might, or goes into the "bridge" position again — fighting for his life while Nurse Lucrezia and Adolf hold him down.

VIVALDI *(continuing)*: We once again register a classic deviant symptom: the patient has no sense of security. Note that! *(Nurse Lucrezia and Adolf brutally force A to lie motionless.)* Mr. Forgetmenot, do you want so much to return to that comfy little isolation-cell of yours? To be alone a little?

PATIENT A: *Yes!!*

VIVALDI: As you see, a blatant asocial disposition... lacks confidence in his environment... Would anyone like to ask a question or two before my distinguished colleague now gives the injection?

He nods politely and pleasantly to Fortinbras and lifts the sheet a little while pointing to the belly of the patient.

A female medical student in the audience, ADELAIDE, raises her hand.

ADELAIDE: Professor, could it be that he just likes to sleep on his tummy?

VIVALDI: *Li... li... li... likes!!*

ADELAIDE: Yes... uh... maybe he doesn't really mean any-thing... by it... doesn't have bad intentions... but he just likes it... and likes to be alone, I mean... you know, to walk around like that... by himself...

FORTINBRAS: Stand up! *(She stands.)* Who are you? And what are you doing here?

ADELAIDE: Uh... uh... A... Adelaide... medical student, born in Winkelsspfuhl... 19 years old... schizoid... appendix removed at age 11... The good of the community before the good of the individual! As everybody knows, the alleged harmful effects of nuclear weapons are grossly exaggerated!

FORTINBRAS: "Likes!" You are a student, what do you mean by "likes?" Huh?!

ADELAIDE: Uh... uh... I, I meant... nothing maybe... just that, you know...

FORTINBRAS: "You know," "uh," "uh," "you know..." What?! Do you have your dossier and summary with you? Of course, you meant something by what you said.

Adelaide in a panic puts her hand to her throat and holds out a tag hanging on a thin chain.

ADELAIDE: Here is my tag!

Vivaldi points to Patient A and signs that he is to be anaesthetized immediately and placed over on the dissecting table. Fortinbras leans over A, pulls Adolf aside and whispers a few words to him, whereupon Adolf looks at Adelaide and then at the exit, not letting go of her with his eyes. Fortinbras holds Patient A's feet tight with the weight of his own body, then leans over him and with great force pushes the syringe up under the sheet. Patient A strains and stretches with all his might in the most terrible convulsions, screams loudly once and suddenly falls lifeless down on the table. Nurse Lucrezia lifts him by herself over onto the dissecting table, where he lies as if dead. Vivaldi meanwhile has taken over the interrogation of Adelaide.

VIVALDI: Pardon me, little Miss Adelaide, but be quite calm now, little lady... Relax completely and feel at ease. Breathe deeply a few times now and don't tighten your muscles... that's it, that's better. And now, just answer my question frankly and openly. *Do you yourself sleep on your stomach?*

Adelaide, frightened, looks around and then runs for her life towards the exit, which is cut off by Adolf. She turns and runs through the auditorium towards the door of the polyclinic and the cold-storage room. Nurse Lucrezia and Adolf carry her squirming over to the table where Patient A has been lying.

VIVALDI: Now, Miss Adelaide, strip from the waist up.
ADELAIDE: *No!!*

He nods to Nurse Lucrezia, who wrenches the sweater off of her.

VIVALDI: Thank you, Nurse! Now listen here, little Miss Adelaide, has it been a long time that you have felt isolated and alienated among your friends and other students? *(Pause.)* Perhaps you don't like to answer questions? *(Pause. To the audience.)* As you can see, a highly developed syndrome: a) underdeveloped adaptability, b) infantile attitudes of negativism, c) development of Angst, d) emotional coldness, e) lack of contact and f) does not answer questions. We are confronted with an entirely asocial human being — based on poorly developed and permanently impaired mental faculties. Can any of the fellow students and close friends of the subject of the experiment here present — or shall we say of patient B — complete the profile of social disease by their own observations of further deviations in the subject's pattern of behavior?

FEMALE STUDENT: Maidenhead intact. Sleeps on her stomach.

VIVALDI: Aha! *Virgo intacta!* Well, well, well! So that's it.

Dr. Vivaldi
One of the author's sketches for the play.

SCENE C

NURSE: We have here before us Case No. 3 in the series of experiments: Adelaide, who also went through a successful normalization — *or so it seems.*

ADELAIDE *(alone. Gets up)*: It's a couple of years ago now. *(Someone knocks on the door.)* Gottfred was so kind. But he wasn't getting along too well, and he sometimes walked about in a dreamworld of his own. He sometimes got completely carried away. I have never met a boy as kind as Gottfred. *(Someone knocks on the door.)* Is that... is that... you? Gottfred? Come in!

GOTTFRED *(enters)*: Hi, Adelaide!

ADELAIDE: Hello, Gottfred! *(Pause.)*

GOTTFRED: It's so nice here in your room.

ADELAIDE: Do you really think so?

GOTTFRED: Yes, very nice — really!

ADELAIDE: It was nice of you to come.

GOTTFRED: Do you really think so?

ADELAIDE: Yes very nice — really! *(Pause.)*

GOTTFRED: And there's your bed. That's a pretty bedspread you've got.

ADELAIDE: Do you think so?

GOTTFRED: Yes — very nice, really. Is it nice and soft?

ADELAIDE: Oh, not too bad. But it isn't healthy to have it too soft. You can feel it if you like.

GOTTFRED *(feeling the bed with his hand)*: It's very nice and soft.

ADELAIDE *(points)*: That's me in that picture when I was a kid.

GOTTFRED: That's very cute.

ADELAIDE: No, I think I look like a sausage.

GOTTFRED: All little kids do. They're supposed to look like sausages. But it's cute anyway. For such a little kid, it's very cute.

ADELAIDE: And that picture over there, that's my mom and dad when they were young.

GOTTFRED: That's a beauty! Your mother was very pretty — almost as pretty as you are.

ADELAIDE: She was much prettier.

GOTTFRED: Your father is very handsome too in that picture. Solid. He looks like a real *man*. And the uniform really looks good on him.

ADELAIDE: He's still very strong and athletic.

GOTTFRED: I'm not strong or athletic...

ADELAIDE: Why should that matter?

GOTTFRED: Do you really think it doesn't?

ADELAIDE: Of course, I do.

GOTTFRED: That it doesn't matter at all?

ADELAIDE: Yes, 'cause you've got so many other good qualities.

GOTTFRED: I wish I also were strong and athletic like that. I'm terrible at gym and sports.

ADELAIDE: But that's not what matters most of all.

GOTTFRED: The others often laugh at me.

ADELAIDE: I'll never laugh at you.

GOTTFRED: For sure?

ADELAIDE: I swear. Never. There are a lot of guys who laugh at me too. At the things I say and...

GOTTFRED: Don't let it bother you. I'll never laugh at you. *(Pause.)* You're the only friend I have.

[99]

ADELAIDE: And you're the only friend I have.

GOTTFRED: Do you know that practically all people betray each other?

ADELAIDE: Yes, I've heard about it. *(Sits on the bed.)* Everybody says it should be that way. The good of the community before the good of the individual... everybody should betray each other, and we should love the government and our country above all other things. In the Women's Youth League we learn how... to tell everything about our friends.

GOTTFRED: That's how it is with us too... in the Patriotic Front for Young Men... We have to tell everything to the group leader. *(Sits down next to her.)* But I'll never betray you.

ADELAIDE: And I'll never betray you.

GOTTFRED: Shall we promise each other?

ADELAIDE: Yes, we'll never betray each other.

GOTTFRED: Now we have something no one else knows about.

ADELAIDE: Yes.

GOTTFRED: We'll always be faithful.

Adelaide puts her head on his shoulder. He puts his arm around her, and they remain sitting like that. He kisses her, and it develops into a very tender, very chaste and shy love scene. The door suddenly opens, and Adelaide's parents come in, talking in loud voices. They notice all of a sudden that Gottfred is there.

DAD: Well, well, well! Excuse us! We had no idea you had company!

Gottfred jumps up and bows. The two adults are noisy and loud the whole time.

MOM: No, we really had no idea.

DAD: We *really* didn't mean to disturb you!

MOM: So nice to see you, Gott! *(Takes his hand.)* Very nice.

DAD *(shakes Gottfred's hand)*: It's awfully nice to see you! Awfully nice.

MOM: Well, it's very nice and private in here, isn't it?

DAD: You mustn't let yourselves be disturbed by us! *(Smiles.)*

MOM: No, don't let us disturb you! Just have a good time together, the two of you.

DAD: I do hope we haven't disturbed you — and that you'll continue to have a good time.

MOM: And I'm sure you'll take good care of yourselves, won't you? You will take care?

GOTTFRED: Oh, yes! Yes.

MOM: I'm sure you have a sense of responsibility...? *(Smiles.)*

DAD: Just make sure it doesn't affect your homework — your schoolwork.

MOM: Yes, because your schoolwork comes before everything else.

DAD: Well, we'll leave you now. We won't disturb you! But remember your homework!

ADELAIDE: We were just thinking about going out a bit.

DAD *(always overly jovial and loud in his friendliness)*: Yessirree — that's the thing — fresh air, now that is something one can't do without!

MOM: Oh, yes, fresh air. But don't forget your schoolwork.

DAD: You know: Duty first, and pleasure afterwards. *(Smiles.)*

MOM: Bye now, children!

DAD *(very heartily)*: Come back whenever you like, Gottfred! Bye, bye!

Mom and Dad leave. Adelaide and Gottfred try to pick up where they left off, but it doesn't work. It's ruined. Adelaide is almost in tears and hides her face. She's afraid, and Gottfred is anxious and unsure of himself.

ADELAIDE: Come on, let's go out for a walk.

GOTTFRED: Yes, let's go.

They go out.

ADELAIDE: I'm sick of all this. It's so dumb.

GOTTFRED: I'm sick of it all too. I hate both school and the Patriotic Front for Young Men. *(They sit down on a bench.)* I'd like to run away... Shall we run away together, Adelaide... far, far away?

ADELAIDE: Where to?

GOTTFRED: Far away to a place without social police, without disciplinary camps, without the National Youth Front.

ADELAIDE: But there isn't any place like that. The whole world is just like here.

GOTTFRED: They've even poisoned the moon.

ADELAIDE: We can't do anything; there's nowhere to go.

GOTTFRED: We wouldn't even get across the border.

ADELAIDE: The social police would get us right away. They'd test us. We won't get away.

GOTTFRED: But we can be faithful to each other.

ADELAIDE: We'll never betray each other.

GOTTFRED: We'll never betray each other.

*****

[Later: Mom, Dad and Adelaide.]

DAD: I repeat — I don't want to see that boy again! I don't want to see you two together.

MOM: He's not a real *boy*, Adelaide. And he doesn't do well in school.

DAD: He'll never be a *real man*. He's poor in physical education, and he neglects the Patriotic Front for Young Men and the National Youth Front.

ADELAIDE: Why should he have to be a *real man*?

DAD: Because... because... then... then... he'll be a *real man*! Is that clear enough? Is that an answer for you?

ADELAIDE: No. I don't think that's any answer — that he must be a real man, because then he'll be a real man.

DAD: Listen to that! She is influenced by him already!

MOM: You are never to see him again! He's lazy and useless.

DAD: I've found out about him: He's an outsider. He goes around by himself. And God knows what kind of thoughts he has. He belongs in a disciplinary camp.

ADELAIDE: But I like him.

MOM: You *like* him!

DAD: She *likes* him — that abnormal creep! She *likes* that asocial outsider! We'll put an end to *that*! That fairy!

MOM: Couldn't you have found a healthy and normal friend? Oh, dear God! Why must it be *our* daughter who is different from others? When there are so many healthy, normal, fine boys? And the neighbors...

DAD: I should certainly like to know what you talk about when you're alone! I'm sure he has abnormal opinions on everything — thinks differently from ordinary people, doesn't he!?

ADELAIDE: That's why I care for him.

MOM: *Care for!* Oh, Jesus Christ! *(Cries.)* Cares for... I hope at least you're careful.

ADELAIDE: Yes. Nobody knows what we talk about.

MOM: I mean *careful*... show a sense of responsibility.

ADELAIDE: In what way?

DAD: Don't pretend you don't understand. Mom means that she hopes you've been using contraceptives.

ADELAIDE: No, that's something we've never used.

MOM: Oh, my God! God Almighty, they haven't used contraceptives! Don't you ever think of us! What if...

DAD *(furious)*: You've never used contraceptives? That's the most egotistical thing I've ever heard in my life! The crudest and most egotistical...

MOM *(crying)*: And that's the thanks we get for all we've done for you! *(Furious.)* Why haven't you used contraceptives?

DAD: Answer your mother when she talks to you! Why haven't you used contraceptives?

ADELAIDE: It isn't necessary.

MOM: Ungrateful child! What will the neighbors say?

DAD: You are really a couple of pigs! Only thinking of yourselves! Didn't you learn at school how to take care of yourself?

MOM: And you don't even care how we feel, just because its better without!

DAD: And you're supposed to be our daughter! Doing it without contraceptives — you're like two animals! After all we've done for you! *Like animals!*

MOM *(crying)*: You ought to be ashamed of yourself...

ADELAIDE: It isn't necessary because we've never been together that way.

DAD *(barking, staccato)*: What?! What?! What?!

MOM: What *are* you saying?

ADELAIDE: We've never been together that way.

DAD: She's a liar too!

MOM: An ungrateful liar!

ADELAIDE: No, it's true! We've never been together like that.

DAD *(hits his forehead)*: Then he really is abnormal! *(More and more suspicious.)* What have you been doing then?

MOM *(crying and snivelling)*: Unnatural and abnormal. And that's *my* daughter!

ADELAIDE: We talk.

DAD: In that case — I know I did the right thing. Talk!

ADELAIDE: What have you done?

DAD *(triumphantly)*: I'll tell you what! I have reported Gottfred to the National Youth Front and to the Juvenile Department of the Social Police.

ADELAIDE: Reported Gottfred?

She bows her head and says no more.

*****

[Later: Officer II, FEMALE OFFICER and Adelaide.]

ADELAIDE *(exhausted, broken)*: Let me sleep!

FEMALE OFFICER: You must understand that when it's your own father who has reported you, then it's a serious matter. Now tell us everything!

OFFICER II: You're neglecting the schedule, you've neglected the Youth League for Women and you've been going with an outsider, a boy who will never be a *real man*.

FEMALE OFFICER: Your own mother has also reported you. Tell us *all* you know about Gottfred!

ADELAIDE: I'm so tired. Let me go. Let me sleep!

FEMALE OFFICER: You'll get to sleep, when you have told the truth.

ADELAIDE: Let me sleep first.

Adelaide totters unsteadily.

FEMALE OFFICER: Let's have no emotionalism here. *(Gives her a chair.)* Sit down!

Adelaide sits down and immediately falls asleep. The Female Officer pulls the chair out from under her. Both Officers laugh at her lying asleep on the floor. They lift her up.

ADELAIDE: Mommie! *(Waking up.)* Let me sleep!

OFFICER II: We'll keep you awake ten days more if necessary. Tell the truth and you'll get to sleep as long as you want.

ADELAIDE *(crying)*: I don't know anything about him. He's kind.

FEMALE OFFICER: What does "kind" mean? What do you mean by that word?

ADELAIDE: Just that he's good and gentle...

OFFICER II: Why did you use the word "kind"? *Why?*

FEMALE OFFICER: Would you like to know where he is now?

ADELAIDE *(almost awake)*: Yes!

FEMALE OFFICER *(smiles)*: He's in a disciplinary camp.

OFFICER II: And you think he's so *kind!* He's stubborn, disobedient and callous. *(Adelaide lowers her head and is silent.)* Tell me, what were you two doing together?

ADELAIDE: We were together because we liked each other, just like everyone else.

FEMALE OFFICER: Did you have sexual intercourse?

ADELAIDE: Yes.

OFFICER II: How often?

ADELAIDE: Every time we met.

FEMALE OFFICER: *That's a lie!*

ADELAIDE: No, it's true! We always had... sexual intercourse. That's why we met.

FEMALE OFFICER *(smiles)*: You're lying, my dear. It says on your card that you have preserved your maidenhood — *virgo intacta*!

OFFICER II: You've kept your chastity, my girl!

ADELAIDE: That's not true. It was just something I said at home.

FEMALE OFFICER: It's easy to check that.

She grabs Adelaide around the arms from behind and holds her tight, then forces her to her knees and bends her upper body backwards.

OFFICER II: Regular routine check?

FEMALE OFFICER: Yes.

Officer II bends over Adelaide and carries out the examination. She screams and struggles with all her might. He takes his time and inspects her conscientiously, then gets up.

OFFICER II: Virgin.

FEMALE OFFICER: It's an open and shut case. *(Lets Adelaide go; she remains huddled up on the floor, sobbing.)* She was lying to us the whole time. Get up!

ADELAIDE *(remaining on the floor)*: Leave me alone.

They get her up. She's shaky on her legs.

FEMALE OFFICER: You have lied and lied and lied! Tell
the truth and you'll be left alone... You'll get to sleep as
long as you want...

OFFICER II: What did you two do together?

FEMALE OFFICER: We haven't even started to get tough
with you. But if you don't tell us the truth now, you're
going to get a taste of what it means to put yourself outside of society.

OFFICER II: When you've told the truth, you may go home.

ADELAIDE: I don't want to go home. Never!

FEMALE OFFICER: You want to study medicine?

ADELAIDE: Yes.

She is on the verge of a breakdown.

FEMALE OFFICER: We'll see to it that you're allowed to
study, if you tell the truth now.

OFFICER II: What did you talk about?

ADELAIDE: Leave me alone.

FEMALE OFFICER: We are going to keep on with you until
you don't even know your own name.

She sakes her violently.

ADELAIDE: Gottfred...

*She falls in a heap on the floor. They lift her up. She is like a wet
lump.*

FEMALE OFFICER: What did Gottfred say to you?

ADELAIDE: ...that everyone betrays each other and that...

FEMALE OFFICER: And that...?

ADELAIDE: ...that he detested the National Youth Front...

OFFICER II: Aha! That's it! And...?

ADELAIDE *(half asleep)*: ...that he... that we should run away... go away together, far, far away... away from all the surveillance police and the Youth Front... that we should never betray each other.

FEMALE OFFICER: Perfect. We'll keep a record of that.

OFFICER II *(to audience)*: But Adelaide's normalization was not one-hundred percent. *Now* she is truly exposed!

*****

[Return to the lecture.]

VIVALDI: AHA! — Marvelous observation! *Virgo intacta*, sleeps on her stomach! Thank you, thank you! Oh, do undress her below too, Nurse!

A violent, acrobatic fight begins between Nurse Lucrezia and Adelaide, Adelaide resisting with desperate strength and courage. Nevertheless, she is stripped of her clothes item by item until finally she has only her panties on, possibly nothing.

VIVALDI *(continuing)*: As you know, social surgery places the freedom and dignity of the individual above all other considerations. *(Leans over Adelaide.)* Have you had problems with your bowel movements in childhood? *(To the audience.)* Many young women are deviants on this important point, please note, and do not stick to the hours fixed specifically for this purpose. *(To Adelaide, threatening.)* Fixed hours! Have you had irregular defecation?

ADELOIDE *(in fear of death)*: No, no, no!

STUDENTS: She has been observed! She has constipation!

Fortinbras comes closer with the syringe.

VIVALDI: Well, then! Show her the syringe, Your Honor, Supreme Court Surgeon! *(To Adelaide.)* What did you mean by saying that the subject of experiment No. 1 perhaps "just liked to walk around by himself like that?" Do *you* happen to know what he was *thinking about* when he was walking about like that? What?! — Relax completely now, my dear! We're all so fond of you here... What did you mean by that?

ADELAIDE *(broken, weak, lets all hope fly)*: I... felt sorry for him... He was so small and looked so kind... *(Pause.)*

VIVALDI *(extremely gently and kindly)*: Do you still feel sorry for him, my dear?

ADELOIDE *(aggressively): No! As everybody knows, the alleged harmful effects of nuclear weapons are grossly exaggerated.*

VIVALDI *(as before)*: Do you still think he looks kind?

ADELOIDE *(shaking her head frantically)*: No!!

VIVALDI: You may certainly sleep on your stomach, my dear. Turn around, if you like.

ADELOIDE *(in a panic, lifting her head in desperation and trying to get loose)*: No, no, no!!... not on my stomach!!

VIVALDI: Put her on her stomach! *(Nurse Lucrezia and Adolf turn Adelaide over by twisting her arms and legs. She is still resisting when Vivaldi with great accuracy puts the tip of his finger on her spine.)* Here, Professor! Right in between the eighth and the ninth vertebrae!

Deep, complete silence. Fortinbras raises the syringe while Vivaldi washes the spot in alcohol. Adelaide cries and whimpers. Fortinbras gives the injection, quick and firm; at the same moment Adelaide lets out a piercing scream, short but loud, and twists around a little on the table without anyone holding her. Then she lies lifeless, with hands and feet off the edge of the table.

VIVALDI *(resuming)*: Thank you, dear colleague! Thank you... *(Applause. He nods to everyone.)* Now it is over. *(Wipes the perspiration from his brow.)* Poor dear... and now she'll feel good, so very, very good! Now, ladies and gentlemen, after this interesting case, which we more or less got as a bonus through Patient B, we shall return to our original demonstration. Would Nurse roll out the material, please?

Adolf moves Adelaide to the side while Nurse Lucrezia leads Mr. Forgetmenot to the operating table. He is awake now, but goes along passively after her, without thinking of flight or resistance.

FORTINBRAS: Before we begin the operation, I would like to emphasise most emphatically that it is only the most malignant cases that demand surgical treatment — and only the completely incurable cases that end up as live experimental material to be kept in storage. In this particular case society spent all its resources in the attempt to resocialize the patient into a healthy and normal life, but all in vain. You will now hear the patient's testimony in his own words.

SCENE D

FORGETMENOT: Actually, I managed quite well at school, even though it got difficult in the last couple of years. It wasn't until my military service that I was totally exposed. That's when my diagnosis was made with all its terrible implications, and it was revealed that I was totally useless, completely asocial and incapable of adjusting — worthless and useless both in military and economic terms.

The first symptoms had appeared, however, by my last years at school. I had a strong aversion to anything collective, to collective sports and collective pleasures. Instead of football, I'd rather go for a walk by myself. Instead of the movies I preferred to read a book. These signs of social decay were, of course, observed by my teachers, and the school doctor withdrew my permission-to-be-alone card. They tried through kindness and consideration to make me healthy and normal and useful, and I also did my best to adapt myself. Naturally, it was written both on my dossier and my tag that I showed signs of asocial, deviant and individual behavior, but no one understood how serious these disturbances were. During military service, however, the abnormalities broke out in full bloom: it was traumatic for me to have to eat in the canteen together with the other recruits, and it was disgusting and intolerable to have to share the toilet and shower room with so many people. But the worst was to have to sleep in the barracks together with so many others. The drills were loathsome too and the orders repulsive. In the beginning I was so unhappy with this collective existence I cannot even describe it. But then one night everything changed.

While the others were sleeping, I crept out of the dormitory and into the quiet, slumbering camp. The first time I did this there was even moonlight. I found a hiding place on the outskirts of the camp and sat down. I was all by myself and I felt a tremendous joy in sitting there like that — the dark sky, the stars and the quiet gave me a sensation of peace and security that I had never felt before. In the foliage of the enormous trees I could hear the soft moaning of the wind, and once in a while a bat would flutter past up above. It was marvelous just being there. From that moment a new period of my life began. The more unhappy I was during the day, at mealtime in the canteen, on the drill grounds or in the gym or in the shower room, the happier I would be at night. In this way I led a double life for a long time, and the quiet, lonely nights helped me to endure the days.

[The Social Police step up.]

CAPTAIN: So, we've caught you redhanded. Is this the first time you've been out at night?

FORGETMENOT: Uh... uh... yes... uh-uh.

SERGEANT I: Tell the truth now, or we'll break every bone in your body.

CAPTAIN: Answer!

FORGETMENOT: No, I've been out before.

CAPTAIN: Often?

FORGETMENOT: Yes... every night.

CAPTAIN: What do you do out at night?

FORGETMENOT: Nothing... just look at the trees and the stars.

CAPTAIN: Liar! Pig!

SERGEANT I: Filthy creep!

Sergeant I hits him so that he falls over toward Sergeant II.

SERGEANT II: Pig!

Sergeant II hits him so that he falls back. Sergeant I kicks him down.

SERGEANT I: Tell the truth!

CAPTAIN: What do you do out at night? Get up!

FORGETMENOT: I just go and find myself a place to sit and think...

CAPTAIN: So you want tough treatment, do you? You're begging for a bit of breeding, huh?

The Captain hits him over to Sergeant II, who kicks him in the belly.

SERGEANT II: There's one for you.

Sergeant II kicks him over to Sergeant I, who knocks him down.

SERGEANT I: Get up!

Forgetmenot crawls around on all fours and can't get up.

SERGEANT I *(continuing)*: Stand up!

Sergeant I kicks him. Sergeant II grabs him by the ears and pulls him up.

SERGEANT II: Stand up straight when we're talking to you!

[114]

FORGETMENOT: Oh, my God!

He moans and staggers.

CAPTAIN: What do you do out at night?

FORGETMENOT: Nothing, Captain. I just sit still in peace and quiet, Captain.

CAPTAIN: Oh yes, you'll get your peace and quiet! We'll wipe the floor with you. *(All three stand still and stare at him.)* Tell us who you meet at night!

FORGETMENOT: No one, Captain.

The Captain nods to the Sergeants, who each grab Forgetmenot from behind by one arm and hold him.

CAPTAIN: Every time you lie, you get a kick in the crotch. Understand?

FORGETMENOT: I'm not lying.

The Captain kicks him in the crotch.

CAPTAIN: Like this!

FORGETMENOT *(doubled over in pain)*: Ow... ow!

CAPTAIN: Do you want more?

FORGETMENOT *(gasping for air)*: No, no... for God's sake! Please... please.

CAPTAIN: Then tell us what you did at night.

FORGETMENOT *(weakly)*: I was just out to be alone.

The Captain kicks him in the crotch again.

CAPTAIN: Let him go!

The Sergeants release him, and he falls on the floor in spasms.

CAPTAIN: Hold his arms!

They hold his arms down to the floor, straight out from his sides, so that Forgetmenot lies stretched out on his back. The Captain places one foot on his throat and presses. Forgetmenot tries to breathe, kicks his feet and gives off a few muffled sounds. The Captain takes his foot away.

CAPTAIN: Tell the truth now, or I'll choke you.
FORGETMENOT: I've told you everything... ow... ow... ow...

The Captain again puts his foot on Forgetmenot's throat and presses down until Forgetmenot stops squirming and moving altogether.

CAPTAIN Let him go!

They let him go; he lies motionless.

SERGEANT I: So help me, I think that little idiot was really telling the truth.
CAPTAIN: All the worse for him, if he's walking around alone at night for no reason at all.
SERGEANT II: He seems pretty incorrigible.

Forgetmenot moves, groans and puts his hand to his throat.

SERGEANT I: Is there anything you want?
FORGETMENOT: To be alone... left alone... I haven't done anything to you. *(Cries.)*

CAPTAIN: You're going to a disciplinary camp, and there you won't be let alone for a second.

FORGETMENOT: Oh, no! No! Not a disciplinary camp! Kick me and hit me, do what you want with me, but don't send me there! Oh, please! Let me stay here! I'll do whatever you say!

CAPTAIN: We can't do any more for you. We can't help you any more here.

FORGETMENOT: Oh, dear God! Oh, dear God!

CAPTAIN *(to audience)*: He spent two years in a disciplinary camp, Category B, the toughest one. Then he was discharged, after his country had done all it could to make him into a healthy and normal human being. He also spent long periods in a disciplinary psychiatric isolation ward, where he received, together with other treatment, electroshock. At the time of his discharge he appeared to be one-hundred percent normalized, but it didn't take long before he had his first relapse. The poison was in his blood.

FORGETMENOT *(to audience)*: I could never get those quiet nights out of my mind — when I sat alone outside — and after a while I began to go out in the city at night. I always tried to find a bench in a park where I could be surrounded by trees and see the night sky above me. Sometimes — especially on starlit nights — I would forget everything and feel nothing but an immense joy and quiet, an undreamed of peace and freedom.

Even in the daytime I would sometimes get lost in my dreams, and twice I was hit by traffic while crossing the street. One time this brought about a costly traffic jam, because I ended up lying in the middle of the street after being run over. All of this was recorded on my card.

Three times I was arrested by the Social Police while sitting alone on a park bench at night. And the last time...

*****

[Return to the lecture.]

FORTINBRAS: That, of course, was the last straw: his last chance of becoming a useful, normalized human being. The patience of the government had to be exhausted sometime. He was definitively diagnosed as a totally unsuccessful case, incurably asocial — and therefore transferred to the disciplinary clinic's surgical ward, where he has been stored ever since in a partly anaesthetized, partly deep-frozen state in the cold-storage room for living material. From whence he now rises to provide his country a final and farewell service.

Nurse Lucrezia has prepared a syringe, which Fortinbras uses intramuscularly on Forgetmenot with immediate effect. From this point on, Forgetmenot is unconscious. Vivaldi goes to the dissecting table.

VIVALDI: Ladies and gentlemen, we shall now begin the neuro-plastic operation here prepared, basing it on immutable social-surgical principles.

FORTINBRAS *(furious)*: Now, listen here, dear colleague! I protest against such an obvious example of malpractice! Transplantation of endocrine glands is the only method to consider in this case!

VIVALDI: *I* am the guest lecturer!

FORTINBRAS: I draw to your attention the fact that I am a Nobel Prize laureate! *For peace! (Softly, pleading.)* I want so much to operate.

VIVALDI: I draw to your attention that, in addition to the Pentagon Peace Prize, I also hold the Grand Normalization Prize of the World Health Organisation! And I am invited here to carry out the operation!

FORTINBRAS: As the responsible head of The Surgical Institute for Criminal Justice I cannot allow the operation to be carried out... unless...

He looks at Vivaldi and becomes thoughtful.

VIVALDI: ... we could come to an agreement?

FORTINBRAS: Yes.

He sits down and thinks.

VIVALDI: Let's say you take the glands, and I take the brain mantle.

FORTINBRAS *(gets up and gives him his hand)*: It's a deal!

VIVALDI: I stand by my word.

They shake hands like sportsmen.

FORTINBRAS: Oh, Nurse! Bring the slop buckets here! Put them there, that's it. (*She brings the white plastic buckets with red crosses on them.*) Thank you, thank you! And the instrument table. Thank you, Nurse.

The surgeons choose their instruments, and everything is put in order for an aseptic operation. Vivaldi touches Patient A's forehead with the tip of a glowing instrument and Forgetmenot, who is covered by a large sheet, wriggles in spite of the anaesthetization.

FORINBRAS *(continuing)*: Dear colleague, let us begin.

[119]

He lifts his knife. The lighting is lowered, so that only the operating lamp shines.

VIVALDI: Ready, get set, go!

He puts an electrical drill to Patient A's crown, and a tremendous grinding sound of bone being cut is heard. Fortinbras sets about opening the abdominal cavity.

VIVALDI *(shouting)*: Say, colleague!

FORTINBRAS *(at work)*: Yes?

VIVALDI: Do you remember in the year 1848 when old Professor Langenbeck carried out that thigh-bone amputation in front of a full auditorium at the old Benevolence Hospital in Berlin... the whole operation, including ligation of blood vessels and veins, with skin, muscle and fascia incisions, as well as sawing off the bones, in 37 seconds flat?! What do you say to that?

FORTINBRAS: Nurse Lucrezia! *(Over the tremendous sound of Vivaldi's drill and sawing machine trepanning Forgetmenot's cranium.)* Nurse! The stopwatch is lying on the instrument table.

[Nurse Lucrezia finds the stopwatch and stands ready to count.]

FORTINBRAS *(continuing)*: Before you get through the cranium, colleague, I shall take the thigh bone!

VIVALDI: The bucket, the bucket! *(Something falls into the bucket.)* All right! Now!

Both work like mad. We hear only sounds of tools: hammer, drill and saw. Once in a while a splash is heard in the buckets as parts of Forgetmenot are thrown away one after the other. Adolf runs out with them to the deep-freezing room. A tremendous grinding sound is heard as Fortinbras saws through the thigh bone.

VIVALDI: Stop! Finished!

FORTINBRAS: You win, colleague. But you won't begrudge me a rematch, I trust? Will you take the other thigh-bone amputation while I finish off with the glands?

VIVALDI: With great pleasure!

They change places.

VIVALDI *(continuing)*: Nurse, will you give the signal to start?

NURSE: One-two-three, GO!

They work in silence. Then the sound of Vivaldi's bone saw is heard.

VIVALDI: The slop bucket, Adolf! Quick!

A splash in the bucket. Adolf carries it out.

FORTINBRAS: The bucket, Nurse. *(New splash.)* To the cold storage room!

Splash again. Like two old tailors, they sew up Forgetmenot's thighs and abdominal cavity with long, rhythmical movements of their arms.

FORTINBRAS *(raising his hands)*: Stop! I'm finished!

VIVALDI *(the same)*: Me too!

NURSE: Supreme Court and Disciplinary Surgeon, Professor Fortinbras, M.D. won by two point seven seconds.

Tremendous applause.

VIVALDI: That business with the glands is veterinary science, pure and simple; it has no therapeutic value.

FORTINBRAS *(reproachfully)*: You're a poor loser, dear colleague.

Between the two surgeons all one can see is a lump under the sheet with two arms sticking out. Forgetmenot's trepanned and opened head is covered by a white cloth.

VIVALDI: The terms were unequal. The glands are child's play. But *(pointing to Forgetmenot's arms)* what if we now took an arm each, so that we'll have exactly the same task, and start together? Is it a deal?

FORTINBRAS: Of course! Agreed! Give the signal to start, Nurse.

They move again and take up starting positions.

FORTINBRAS *(continuing)*: Are the slop buckets ready, Adolf?

ADOLF: Yessir, Professor!

NURSE: One-two-three, GO!

Just as before, blows, sawing, bonesawing, but also heavy breathing and gasps from the surgeons who are beginning to get tired. Then two splashes are heard almost simultaneously. Adolf carries the buckets out. The surgeons sew with big, swinging arm movements, quickly and for a long while. Adolf returns.

VIVALDI *(biting off the thread)*: Finished!

FORTINBRAS: Finished!

NURSE: Two tenths in favor of the social surgeon!

FORTINBRAS *(extending his hand)*: Congratulations! *(Applause and stamping of feet from the students.)* What is it, Nurse?

Of Forgetmenot only a big lump is left under the sheet.

NURSE: There seems to be something wrong with the patient; he's not breathing. *(She shakes her head in disapproval.)*

FORTINBRAS: Nothing but a slight indisposition, surely.

He puts his ear to A's chest and listens, while Vivaldi accepts his applause. Fortinbras then draws Vivaldi over to the dissecting table; they both listen, look at each other and shake their heads, shrugging their shoulders.

FORTINBRAS *(continuing)*: He's not breathing.

VIVALDI: Why should he have to breathe?

NURSE: He could have been used over again — at the next demonstration. But now it's too late.

FORTINBRAS *(spreading the sheet up over the corpse's head)*: Oh, dear! Oh, dear! *(Points to the polyclinic.)* Adolf! The deep freeze! Non-living material unit. *(To Nurse Lucrezia.)* And now for Patient B, Nurse. Roll her under the lamp... over here! *(Points. Adelaide is rolled under the lamp. He looks at her, turns to Vivaldi.)* Ah well... Poor little thing! What would you suggest, dear colleague? The glands?

VIVALDI *(pats Adelaide lovingly, gallantly and with obvious flirtation)*: I should have loved to take her along to Bologna... now that spring is here... the spring in Auditorium B on the south side... or to Minsk, when the tulips bloom... *(He breathes deeply and turns to the audience.)* As everybody knows, the alleged harmful effects of nuclear weapons are grossly exaggerated.

He is interrupted by the loud ringing of an electric bell. The students applaud and get up.

NURSE: There will be a forty-five minute break for lunch. Next performance starts at ...

Applause.

— E N D —

Translated by Solrun Hoaas

FROM THE CANBERRA PRODUCTION

I. *Letter to the translator (June 1974)*

Solrun Hoaas
1/14 Northbourne Flats
Braddon, ACT 2601
AUSTRALIA
------------------------   Den 9. juni 1974

Kjære Solrun Hoaas:

           Takk for Deres brev og for interessen for "Amputasjon".
Stykket har ikke tidligere vært oversatt til engelsk, men det har vært spil
over hele Skandinavia - med uroppførelsen i Stockholm, - hvor det faktisk
var en stor suksess. Så vidt jeg kan huske i farten, er ingen av skuespili-
ene oversatt til engelsk, - skjønt jo! I USA er både FUGLEELSKERNE og
TIL LYKKE MED DAGEN! oversatt, men foreløpig ikke oppført. Det har også
vært noe i Irland. Men jeg har hatt så fordømt meget å holde på med de sist
par årene, at jeg har bekymret meg lite om det. Noveller har jeg aldri
skrevet, og av essayene er bare noen ganske få oversatt. Derimot forelig-
ger et par av romanene mine på engelsk (USA), hvor for tiden hele trilogi-
en FRIHETENS ØYEBLIKK, KRUTTÅRNET og STILLHETEN er under oversettelse og
utgivelse.

    Det eneste problem i forbindelse med Deres oversettelse av AMPUTASJON
er at mine engelskspråklige rettigheter henhører under min agent som er
bosatt i New York. Navn og adresse er:

              KURT HELLMER
              Authors' Representative
              52 Vanderbilt Avenue
              New York, New York 10017
              U. S. A.

    Derfor må jeg be Dem om å ta kontakt med ham, og likeledes om å sende
ham en fotokopi av oversettelsen. Naturligvis ville jeg også gjerne selv ha
en kopi, hvis det ikke betyr altfor meget bryderi for Dem.

                        Igjen takk for interessen og for arbeidet
                        med å oversette stykket -

                        Med de hjerteligste hilsener

                              Deres forbundne

                              (Jens Bjørneboe)

[125]

Translation:

June 9th, 1974

Dear Solrun Hoaas:

Thank you for your letter and interest in "Amputation." The play has to date not been translated into English, but it has been performed all over Scandinavia — with the world premiere in Stockholm, — where it was in fact a great success. As far as I can remember offhand, none of the plays have been translated into English, — however, yes! In the USA both *The Bird Lovers* and *Many Happy Returns!* have been translated, but still not performed. There has also been something in Ireland. But I have been so damned busy in the last couple of years that I have not concerned myself much about it. I have never written short stories, and of the essays only very few have been translated. On the other hand, a few of my novels are available in English (USA), where at the moment the entire trilogy *Moment of Freedom*, *Powderhouse* and *The Silence* are in the process of being translated and published.

 The only problem in connection with your translation of *Amputation* is that my English language rights are handled by my agent who lives in New York. His name and adress are:

   KURT HELLMER
   Author's Representative
   52 Vanderbilt Avenue
   New York, New York 10017
   U.S.A.

Therefore I must ask you to contact him, and likewise to send him a photocopy of the translation. Of course, I would also much appreciate receiving a copy, if it is not too much trouble for you.

Again thank you for your interest and work on the translation of the play —

With the most heartfelt greetings

Faithfully yours,
Jens Bjørneboe

II. *Programme notes by the translator (May 1977)*

When he died last year, Jens Bjørneboe was not only a well-established writer and highly polemic social critic, who never let anyone with the label "authority" rest in peace, but he had also become a popular writer — a "distinction" he had never sought.

His seafarer's tale, *The Sharks*, was a runaway bestseller in Norway in 1974 and is now being translated into English. At the time of his death he was due to go to Japan to do research on whaling for another book on that topic.

An essayist, poet, novelist and playwright, he had never previously catered to popular tastes. On the contrary, he often set out to be deliberately provocative, prodding the self-satisfied conscience of a complacent democracy that prides itself on respect for human rights and the freedom of the individual. Rejection of authority is the dominant theme in his writing and anger its dominant mood.

In particular, his essays (published collectively in *Norway, My Norway*, which he referred to as essays about the "guardianship mentality," as well as in *We Who Loved America*), and some of his poetry and plays, like *Amputation* and *The*

[127]

Torgersen Case, give free rein to his biting social satire. *The Torgersen Case* was written in 1973 after one of his many direct involvements with court cases where he saw victimization of the weak by a "justice"-based, almighty power structure — the case of a man convicted of rape-murder on very tenuous grounds in a climate of public hysteria and lynching fervor and kept in jail for over fifteen years.

This was not the first time Bjørneboe confronted the judicial system head-on. His deliberately pornographic novel *Without a Stitch*, written in 1966 to challenge the Norwegian censorship laws, brought him a court case which he lost.

Possibly to keep his anger alive — an anger one senses in almost all of his writing, sometimes to the extent that it overpowers in its immediacy — he refused to forget the war. In his basement he had a large photograph on the wall of young kids hanged during the last world war. For reasons of his own, he chose the same method for his own death. Several of his novels deal with the war, as does much of the poetry, which uses rough cabaret-style rhythm.

This poetry, written in very direct and blunt language, and sometimes with ironic lullaby or marching-song rhythm and Biblical references, at times also reveals a very lyrical side to Bjorneboe's writing and a gentleness in dealing with more personal concerns. He even felt it necessary to apologize for writing poetry in these terms, when his collection of poems, *Ashes, Wind and Earth*, was published (1968): "To concern oneself with poetry today — in a world like ours — gives a feeling of such spiritual luxury, that it demands a defense — an apology." But his poetry, too, is largely a *statement*, and is, as such, consistent with the rest of his work.

In early years he was a school teacher who taught in Rudolf Steiner schools. He lived several years in Germany and spoke fluent German; he also married a German. Aside from translations into other Scandanavian languages, translations into

German predominate, including seven novels and three plays. The novels *Jonas* (1955), *Without a Stitch* (1966), *Moment of Freedom* (1966), *Without a Stitch II* (1968), and the plays *Many Happy Returns!* (1965), *The Bird Lovers* (1966), *Semmelweis* (1969), and *Amputation* (1970) have now been translated into English.

Amputation was first done by the Swedish State Touring Theatre in 1970 in Stockholm; it has since been performed in other Scandinavian countries and recently at the Thesbiteatret, south of Oslo, by Italian director Gianni Lebre, who trained with Peter Brook.

The author's foreword to *Semmelweis*, a play about the Austrian doctor who dared tell established medicos to wash their hands before going from the dissecting ward to the maternity ward, could equally well apply to *Amputation*:

> The authoritarian individual only feels protected and safe as long as it itself is being kicked from above and can also kick downwards; therefore the authoritarian society will always laud obedience as the highest human virtue. The drive to submission to power-hungry authorities is today driving mankind into the greatest catastrophe it has ever experienced.

Be this authority based on wealth, military power, or eloquence.

Solrun Hoaas

III. *Other programme materials*

"This is the world crisis today: that politics have no relation to what is human. The truth is that all our culture, all of European culture, is created by criminals, drunks, syphilitics, the mentally ill, epileptics, narcotic addicts, homosexuals, or at least chronic psychopaths, neurotics and at any rate sufferers from tuberculosis! It is not the so-called healthy forces that create a culture. It is not the skiers and the gym teachers who create a culture. Moreover, in most cases, this 'illness' is healthier than the usual, robust healthiness."

"Just as life itself, culture demands a speck of uncleanliness and at least a minimum of microbes in order to emerge, just as reproduction demands a tiny bit of indecency in order to continue."

"There is no doubt that one of the greatest curses that has devastated European history is our desire to set up an infallible authority, 'the revelation,' the omniscient, the impeccable and the unassailable 'truth,' the basic doctrine which no one must attack, doubt or discuss. Any book which serves to sow doubt and suspicion against infallible doctrines is important and necessary, and a step towards our own liberation."

Jens Bjørneboe
From *We Who Loved America (1970)*

"Robert Liston (1794-1847) of Edinburgh, Scotland, amputated a thigh in 33 seconds. His assistant lost three fingers during the operation."

"The shortest time recorded for a leg amputation in the pre-anaesthetic era was 13 to 15 seconds by Napoleon's Chief Surgeon Dominique Larrey."

The Guiness Book of Records

Amputation (the second version of the play) was premiered in English at the Australian National Theater Arts Centre in Canberra May 10-15, 1977 in conjunction with the Translators Conference and the Australian National Playwrights Conference. Playwright Roger Pulvers directed a cast of six: Ken Gardiner — Dr. Fortinbras, Gary Pritchard — Dr. Vivaldi, Marguerite Wells — Nurse Lucrezia, Harry Schmidt — Adolf, Malcolm Sullivan — Patient A, Marcella O'Hare — Patient B. The Arts Centre space was transformed into a makeshift operating room for the demonstration of Doctors Fortinbras and Vivaldi. This production was also performed at a seminar on Science ad Society, and was attended by 720 doctors and nurses.

IV. *Performance stills*

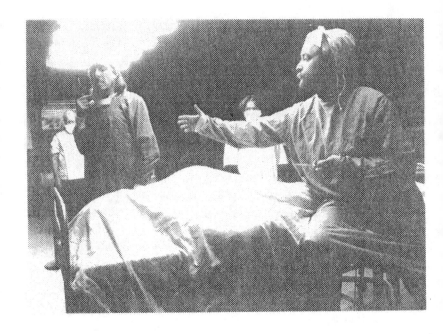

Front: Ken Gardiner (left) as Dr. Fortinbras; Gary Pritchard as Dr. Vivaldi. Back: Harry Schmidt as Adolf; Marguerite Wells as Nurse Lucrezia.

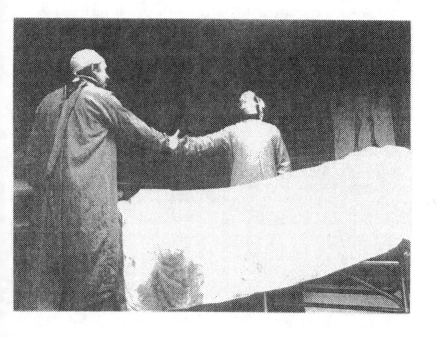

Dr. Fortinbras and Dr. Vivaldi agree to operate. The first will take the glands; the second — the brain mantle.

V. *A review of the production*

Roger Pulvers in Canberra seems to have set out on a one-man crusade to raise the consciousness of theatre people and theatre-going audiences to the work of some of the compelling minds in the contemporary theatre of which we are at present deprived by the language barrier. [...]

For a national translation conference held in Canberra during May, Pulvers introduced to Australian audiences at the Arts Centre, the work of a stark Norwegian writer, Jens Bjorneboe. It is translated into unobtrusive, easily flowing English by Solrun Hoass. Bjorneboe died by his own hand last year. To judge from the brief descriptions available to us of the recurrent theme of social injustice in his work, the anger that informs it and the way he seems to use images of physical violence to demonstrate depredations upon the spiritual nature of man, one gains the picture of a sensitive, Ibsen-like poet with a deep anger against the new and greater inhumanities that have arisen since the time of the great Norwegian dramatist.

A glimpse of the gentleness of Bjorneboe, his poet's joy at the small incidents of nature, his humor and irony, was given at the beginning of the programme with a selection of poems from his collection, *Ashes, Wind and Earth*. A handful of lyrical poems on the natural world is mixed with ironic statements about the good prison life does a man, a nonsense-verse national anthem and a ballad of the north Sea in which a family, faced with the disaster of Father dying at sea, resolves the situation by pickling him in a herring barrel for the rest of the voyage. Too late they discover that the barrel, stamped with the firm's insignia, has been sold along with the rest of the consignment. Sadly they conduct a funeral service over 80 kilos of herring, while on the other side of the world a Hindu is executed for the mysterious murder of a man in a herring barrel.

This latter jovial work is an introduction to his play *Amputation*, which occupies the rest of the evening. There is irony in the play, and grotesquerie: there is also a bitter anger and ugliness.

[Summary of the action.]

Bjorneboe's anger is apparent, but it has the great dramatic saving grace of wit. His points are simple — how the enforcement of majority opinion is the corruption of the sensibilities and how such reinforcement can only be made through fear — and he makes them with the Brechtian method of repetition.

The telling central scene is a moving contract between two virginal teenagers who meet briefly in friendship. Their shy exchanges are brutally interrupted by her parents who cross-examine them on politics and contraceptives. The scene is conducted by the same rules as the surgeons' interrogation of Adolf. In both the betrayal of innocence is complete.

Roger Pulvers has a good team of Canberra actors with which to realize the play. Ken Gardiner and Gary Prichard play the statuesque surgeons; Marguerite Wells, a nice comedy actress, plays Nurse Lucrezia; Harry Schmidt a defeated Adolf and Malcom Sullivan and Marcella O'Hare the touching pair of innocents.

The production is smooth and lucid. I would, however, question Pulvers' decision to excise the grotesque brutalities of the original script, as he describes them, in the interests of our own surviving sensibilities. He claims that kicks in the groin, buckets of blood and severed limbs underneath the operating-table and circular saws in the hands of the surgeons, we would find comic, ineffective and in poor taste. And I am sure we would, as we would find *grand guignol* in poor taste and incredible.

It seems to me, however, that it is the purpose of this angry playwright to offend our taste, to trick us into laughing at horrors, only to turn sick at the implications of our own reaction. In this he has much in common with the post-war generation of German and Eastern European writers, directors, poets and painters, who have attempted through horror and accusation to confront us with that consuming guilt which was Europe's legacy from the Second World War...

Katharine Brisbane
Theatre Australia, July 1977

Oddbjørn Johannessen

Jens Bjørneboe and the Norwegian Theater

Jens Bjørneboe's dramatic works have never received the attention they deserved in Norway. On several occasions in recent years his authorship has been remembered and celebrated. 1995 was an important Bjørneboe year. Then he would have been 75, and the anniversary was celebrated with seminars, book publications and exhibitions. The author, the visual artist and the human being received attention and were debated in the newspapers. The *dramatist* Bjørneboe, however, seemed to have been forgotten — at least by our institutional theaters. The only production of a Bjørneboe drama I registered during the anniversary years was the Thesbiteatret's production of *Amputation* in Tønsberg (Vestfold festival in June). In the fall of 2000 he would have been 80, and spring 2001 was the 25th anniversary of his death. Two more Bjørneboe years. But the situation for his dramatic works was the same as in 1995. This has led me to make some reflections concerning Jens Bjørneboe and the Norwegian teater.

The antipathy toward Bjørneboe the dramatist on the part of the Norwegian theatrical establishment is not of recent date. When he was alive, most established institutions considered him a hair in the soup, and in theatrical circles the myth was created that he was difficult to work with. Of course, he was! Most artists have problems with group dynamics. Yet matters were not so bad as to prevent him from making all the dramas he wrote into collaborative projects. He didn't let go of a single dramatic work before several professional theater folk had been involved in the artistic process and had been allowed a decisive influence on the result. In many ways one can say that few Norwegian dramatists have *collaborated* so intensely as

Jens Bjørneboe. What is particularly striking is that most of his collaborative partners were foreigners. Generally these had in common an engagement in some form of experimental theater — at least measured against the traditions of the Norwegian theater establishment.

However, his first collaborator did belong to the tradition of Ibsen — Helge Krog. Krog understood the dramatic potential latent in the novel *The Evil Shepherd*, and he and Bjørneboe planned a naturalistic theater piece based on raw material from this novel. The collaboration ceased with Krog's death in 1962, but some of his suggestions were included in the final version, *Many Happy Returns!* By the time Bjørneboe took the material up again, he had made contact with the Israeli director Izzy Abrahami, who stood in a wholly different theater tradition. In the printed program of the premiere at Oslo Nye Teater in 1965, Bjørneboe gives Abrahami this mention: "It was Izzy Abrahami who gave me the impetus to rewrite the play in a form which accorded with my own true view of the theater. Sometimes one needs a kick in the rear to actually venture into the water. It was Abrahami who kicked me off the spring-board, and I am very grateful to him for that. A couple of the scenes he himself directly suggested to me."

Several meetings with Bertold Brecht's Berliner Ensemble (the first in the spring of 1959) likewise had a decisive significance both for Bjørneboe's vision of the theater and for his network of professional theater contacts. It caused him, among other things, to insert songs of comment and contrast into both *Many Happy Returns* and his next play, *The Bird Lovers* (1966). The composer for the first play was Finn Ludt, while one of the Berliner Ensemble's "House composers" — Hans Dieter Hosalla — was responsible for the musical side of the original production of *The Bird Lovers* at the National Theater. Hosalla had, among other things, also written music for Brecht's

Arthuro Ui. Another "Berliner," Carl Maria (Charly) Weber, had responsibility for the direction.

Meanwhile yet another foreigner had taken an interest in *The Bird Lovers*, in fact while the piece was still in an outline stage. The Italian-born Eugenio Barba had studied with the Pole Jerzy Grotowski, whose avant-garde theater was located in a town near of Auschwitz. Barba started the Odin Theater in Oslo in 1962, but by 1966 the project was so poorly circumstanced that the operation was moved to Holstebro in Denmark. Barba and the Odin Theater succeeded in putting on their version of *The Bird Lovers* in Oslo — an"adaptation" based on a working draft of the text under the title *The Ornithophiles.* Bjørneboe was both surprised and pleased: "I have worked with directors from Sweden and Israel, and I have always learned something, because the collaboration took place with trust and seriousness. But I have hardly ever gained such a shockingly intense new insight at a performance as at the Odin Theater's version of *The Bird Lovers.* One might almost say a new, *physical* insight." [1]

Bjørneboe kept in touch with Barba after the latter had moved to Denmark, and he was an important conversation partner while Bjørneboe was working on *Semmelweis.* It was Barba who suggested framing this play a prologue and an epilogue set in the present. Another important conversation partner here was the Swedish actor — at that time head of the Scala Theater in Stockholm — Allan Edwall. However, the work on *Semmelweis* shows that Bjørneboe could also collaborate with leading Norwegian theater people. When the play was produced at the National Theater in 1968, it was Magne

---

1. Quoted from "On the Odin Theater's adaptation of *The Bird Lovers*," *On Theater,* Pax 1978. The Swede he refers to here is probably Kåre Santesson, who staged *Many Happy Returns* at the Göteborg Stadsteater in 1966.

Bleness who directed. Otherwise Bjørneboe had scant faith in the Norwegian theater expertise of the time: "Most of the directors I've met know as much about literary dramaturgy as an oyster knows about skiing." [2] But on principle he was for collaboration: "All artists need help from outside." His trust in the Norwegian theater establishment was of course not enhanced when the chief of the National Theater, Erik Kristen-Johanssen, declined an invitation from the biennial International Theater Festival in Venice to participate with *The Bird Lovers* in the fall of 1967.

A sketch of *Amputation* (1970) had been published in the magazine *Ordet* in 1964, but turned into a stage piece only when the leader of the Friteatren in Sweden, Martha Vestin, approached him in 1969 to ask if he had anything she could use. And when the play was ready to be performed, it was as a result of teamwork. The production got very good reviews in the Swedish and Danish press, but was as good as passed over in silence in the dramatist's homeland. Teamwork was also the modus operandi in 1973 when Helge Reistad and the ensemble of Scene 7 staged *The Torgersen Case*, based on the documents from the trial of Frederik Fasting Torgersen, the most talked-about criminal case of the day. Scene 7 was also the arena for the last play Jens Bjørneboe managed to finish, *Blue Jeans: A Collage about Big Business and the Life of a Marketer* (produced in late fall 1974; published in book form 1976).

This quick survey of some of the dramatist Bjørneboe's most important working partners should show that he did not regard his own texts as final. He permitted others to "tinker" with them, provided they were masters of their profession. Several statements indicate that he considered most Norwegian directors either too hung up on tradition or too market-oriented. However, he was reacting not only on his own ac-

---

2. "On the Odin Theater's adaptation of *The Bird Lovers*."

count. He was concerned about the conditions being offered to young dramatists. The institutional theater's main stages were closed to experiments. In an interview in *Fædrelandsvennen* (May 10, 1969) he expresses himself in strong and unequivocal language about Norwegian theater politics: "I am concerned about the tendency for the small stages to become 'cabaretized,' while the main stages are 'musicalized.' Unfortunately things seem to be developing in that direction. The theaters do their duty by the young and by national drama by letting them into the cheap small stages in the amphitheater. That way one gets what one wants: text-writers who can put together sketches, little songs, while the public sits gratefully in a little flock and is content with what it gets... That is deadly dangerous. The writer is never put to the test."

And so what happens on the main stages?

Oh, you know — "the imported, ready-made theater successes, traded through agents and chosen according to how long they have run in New York, London or Moscow."

There is nobody who gambles on new, Norwegian drama. That is too risky. The market rules. That is Bjørneboe's summing-up, and he sees only one way out of dead water: "With all respect for the small stages and experimental theaters, I feel convinced that we cannot have any national drama unless a place is made for it on the main stages. We must do that — that is what those stages are for!"

Since 1969 Bjørneboe himself has been largely relegated to little theaters, insofar as he has been played at all. And it is the amateur theaters which have found him interesting (with the exception of Norwegian Broadcasting's radio and television theater). It is a paradox that the Norwegian dramatist who more than anyone else in the postwar period has written dramas which have aroused interest abroad, who wrote excitingly and insightfully about theater theory, and who was unusually well oriented about what was happening in the international theater world, has become such a stepchild here at home.

Of course, it may be objected — and rightly so — that his plays are not flawless, but his material affords great possibilities for directors and actors. Note his own statement on several occasions: "My plays are *scores* for performance."

Besides, every institutional theater with respect for itself and its own role surely has a cultural duty which transcends the given theater chief's personal taste and opinion.

Nor would it surprise me if the dramatist Bjørneboe could become a box-office success (and here I speak *as a philologist*, to twist Piccolino's well-known words in *The Bird-Lovers* a bit). It appears that he still has the ability to engage young people. In high school and college, for example, he is one of the most popular subjects for term papers in literature.

Regardless, any problems of working with him have long since become passe. The *man* Jens Bjørneboe has now been dead and buried for twenty-six years. The excuses become poorer and poorer.

Translated by Esther Greenleaf Mürer

Esther Greenleaf Mürer

Mad Scientists and Moral Outrage:
The Genesis of Jens Bjørneboe's *Amputation*

1.

*A*mputation builds on a theme which had haunted Jens Bjørneboe from the very beginning of his writing career. To Bjørneboe, authoritarian social structures are a central manifestation of human evil. In two plays — one at the beginning of his career, one toward the end — he uses medical experimentation on unwilling human subjects to illustrate the complicity of modern science in maintaining those structures. *Amputation* — like his first play, *Ere the Cock Crows* — takes aim at perversions of the empirical spirit which exploit or victimize others for purposes of prestige, power and social control; which treat concrete human beings as abstractions, means to an end, obstacles to be overcome.

Bjørneboe belonged to a generation deeply affected by the horrors of Nazi Germany. In several of his works he describes the shock he received as a young, unprepared teenager upon reading Wolfgang Langhof's *Die Moorsoldaten*, an account of one of the first Nazi concentration camps which appeared in Norwegian translation in 1935. He subsequently spent much time in Germany and was profoundly and positively influenced by such great spirits as Goethe, Rilke, Hölderlin, Novalis, Lichtenburg, Meister Eckhardt, Jacob Boehme, Rudolf Steiner and Max Stirner; but his attitude toward Germany remained intensely ambivalent.

During a visit to Germany in 1947 he chanced to acquire documents from the trial of Dr. Sigmund Rascher, a doctor involved in medical experiments on humans, and fortuitously came into contact with members of Rascher's family. The first fruit of this experience was a feature article in the Oslo newspaper *Aftenposten* (November 20,1948), "From Doctor to Executioner in the Name of the Swastika." An expanded version, "The Unbelievable," appeared the following year in the journal *Spektrum.*

Bjørneboe begins by arguing that we can only come to terms with Nazism by analyzing it, understanding its causes and transforming it into constructive experience and insight. Using German sources, Bjørneboe lists three main functions of the camps: as a source of cheap labor, a gathering-place for those who were to be used for medical experiments or exterminated and a training-ground for new executioners. His exposition of the latter point foreshadows the figures of Adolf and Lucrezia in *Amputation:*

> Here the perfect executioner could be hardened and trained; the concentration camps offered the milieu and the human material which was necessary not only to let the inherent bestiality in man have free rein, but to actually cultivate and exercise it. In these training reserves was created the wholly dehumanized being... needed to make the SS into an error-proof instrument, a fully obedient and consistent apparatus of terror which shrank from no action and was deterred by no inhibitions. In the SS Death Squads the new human was born, the human who is not bound by sentimentality or irrational propaganda of compassion... [1]

---

1. Jens Bjørneboe, "Det Utrolige." *Spektrum: litteratur, kunst, samfunnsspørsmal* (1949), No. 2, 101-111. The article, which does not appear in Bjørneboe's collected essays, is discussed at length in Sigurd

A detailed overview of the medical experiments follows. Bjørneboe then focuses on the intellectual milieu from which Nazism sprang — the Western scientific heritage:

> The National Socialist leaders were children of their time and to the degree that they were intellectuals, they were filled with the ideas which have controlled the tone-setting intellectual and scientific milieu in Europe and America for the past 50 years. The doctors and scientists had been marked by the official scientific ways of thinking, and the other, less academic or disciplined minds which took part in the Hitler regime's genesis and development had more popular ideas of the same origin.
> And what kind of ideas were these?
> The most striking thing about the thousands of universities which are spread over the European and the American continents, are that they are all split in two, into a rational and an irrational division, into the natural science faculties on the one hand and the theological-humanist-philosophical on the other. In one you get knowledge; in the other, faith. Natural science has dissociated itself from the religious, the ethical and the philosophical, it no longer feels itself connected with this side of the world...
> The essence of natural science is that everything which honest empirical research... has ascertained —

Aa. Aarnes, "'The Problem of Evil': Nazism in Jens Bjørneboe's writing," translated by John Weinstock. In *The Nordic Mind: Current Trends in Scandinavian Literary Criticism*, ed. by Frank Egholm Andersen and John Weinstock (Lanham MD: University Presses of America, 1986), 223-250. Also online in *Jens Bjørneboe in English*: <http://emurer.home.att.net/about/aarnes1.htm>

it all indicates that the human being is a higher mammal. What we call ethics can only find its basis in respect to social usefulness...

Now suppose that we come into a situation where it obviously serves no useful purpose to be moral. Suppose, for example, that it could be to a nation's advantage to keep a solid stock of slaves of a few million, or that the society would gain from exterminating useless lives, that there would be profit in performing certain experiments or vivisection on criminals. And then suppose that no traditional statutes prevent anyone from doing that. (It was of great significance to the SS doctors in the camps that the SS lawyers in Berlin had put the judicial foundation in order.) Who then can really have any grounds for objecting to higher mammals experimenting with each other? Let us further suppose that one truly took advantage of the modern possibilities for doing away with irrational inhibitions and bourgeois prejudices and that one day there appeared personalities who had the courage and power to think all these thoughts to the end and bring them to actuality. It is not even necessary to ask what would then confront us. *Neither the idea of euthanasia nor that of vivisecting criminals has its origin or its sole defenders among National Socialists.* It will always be to National Socialism's credit that right before our eyes it drew the conclusions of our view of life. It has captured a realization for us...

The German concentration camps carried biological utilitarianism to its logical conclusion in every respect to strengthen one particular race economically, politically and hygienically. We must come to terms with the fact that the camps would never have been thinkable without modern science's concept of the human essence as a biological species. And so we really need not be amazed that when certain thoughts are planted in people, they will sooner or later come to yield consequences. (108f)

At the time this essay was written, Bjørneboe was immersed in Anthroposophy, the "spiritual science" of Rudolph Steiner. Although he later abandoned the anthroposophical path, Bjørneboe remained unshakably opposed to materialistic interpretations of human nature — a fact which kept him perpetually at odds with the radical intelligentsia of his time and place who should have been his natural allies.

Bjørneboe next used the material about the medical experiments as the basis for a play. After it was refused by the Studio Theater (Oslo) in 1950, he added new material and rewrote it as a novel, *Ere the Cock Crows*, which was published by Aschehoug in 1952. Dedicated to "to the memory of the victims of the blindness of heart and coldness of mind which have long characterized modern science," it dissects the ethical schizophrenia which enables the scientist, Dr. Reynhardt (modeled on Rascher), to maintain the illusion that his experiments are "pure science" and "totally apolitical" as he gradually yields to pressure to use his scientific prestige to serve the purposes of the SS propaganda apparatus.

The novel adds a frame to the original play, including two introductory chapters set in 1947 — a first-person narrative based on Bjørneboe's own experience.[2] The narrator, a Norwegian journalist sojourning in Germany, comes into contact with a network of relief workers; with the SS henchman Max

---

2. The original play version is lost. My remarks on the play as opposed to the novel are based on my own reconstruction, which I believe is well supported by the internal evidence of the novel.

— a victim of the dehumanization process described above, now a cripple bedridden in an attic; and with Reynhardt's widow and son. Gradually he pieces together a story which is then told in flashback in the rest of the novel.

A meditation by the narrator in chapter 2 sounds a theme which Bjørneboe was to work out in *Amputation* nearly 20 years later:

> The future will know only two ways of dying. One will be the anonymous, pain-free hospital death. The other will be to perish as an involuntary guinea pig for science, for holy medicine. We still have a period of grace, a few years perhaps, and then it will be past. Never again will anyone die the way my grandfather did. Never again will anyone die as nobody on earth has ever died before...
>
> The corpse factories and the big mass crematoria from the camps are transitional forms — stages on the way from the captain's deathbed to the future's departments for death assistance. You'll be able to die rationally in the future; free of pain — with a film showing and to soothing, state-controlled music, designed for deathbeds. Anonymously, quietly, *without being aware of it*. And without being a burden to friends or relatives. It will be a hygienic, humane process, just as natural as television and cancer. All this will be ours if we're among the constructive, positive citizens of society. In the opposite case — if one belongs to the enemies of society — one will be placed at science's disposal as a research subject.

These are thoughts which are older than National Socialism.[3]

In an afterword to PAX Forlag's 1967 reissue of *Ere the Cock Crows*, Bjørneboe says wryly: "The author can rejoice that the book has not succumbed to death after 16 years. *Alas:* In many respects the book is *more* relevant today than when I began the work." (188)   He cites the British doctor Maurice H. Pappworth's book *Human Guinea Pigs* (London: Routledge & Kegen Paul, 1967) and Henry Knowles Beecher's paper "Ethics and clinical research" (*New England Journal of Medicine,* 1966), both of which report ongoing research on nonconsenting human subjects, including retarded children and mental patients. (189-191)

By this time Bjørneboe has come to regard the bombings of Hiroshima and Nagasaki as experiments comparable to those of the Nazi doctors.   In the same afterword (188f) he cites David Horowitz and the the German journalist and futurist Robert Jungk, whose books — respectively *The Free World Colossus* and *Brighter than a Thousand Suns* — he had reviewed elsewhere,[4] in support of the idea that the use of the bombs was unnecessary to winning the war and that the two cities had been deliberately spared conventional bombing attacks so that scientists and doctors could observe the effects of the atomic

---

3. Bjørneboe, *Før Hanen Galer* (Oslo: Pax, 1967), 57-58.   All references to *Ere the Cock Crows* are to this edition.

4. Bjørneboe, "Atombombens genesis," *Bøker og Mennesker* (Oslo: Gyldendal, 1979), 145-147, is a review of Robert Jungk's *Heller als tausend Sonnen* (1956) which first appeared in *Aftenposten,* 6 November 1957.   A review of David Horowitz's *The Free World Colossus,* dated 1965, appears in the collection *Vi som elsket Amerika* (Oslo: Pax, 1970), 15-18, under the title "Herre Jesus, for en fred!"

bombs. (Bjørneboe states that two different types of bombs were used — one with uranium, one with plutonium — but his source for this point is unclear.) He concludes, "Thereby in a classical sense the conditions were systematically set up for a *scientific experiment on human beings...* It was not just physicists, but doctors too who profited from the experiments: they learned a bit about the effects of radioactive materials."

This theme also appears in *Moment of Freedom* (1966):

> That the American research was regarded as exempt from punishment, while the Germanic and Central Teutonic researches were regarded as punishable, naturally had a morally catastrophic effect on the respect one would otherwise have accorded the conviction of the German scientists.
>
> The only explanation of the differing judgments passed on the two otherwise equivalent types of experiments must be derived from the only real difference between them: namely that whereas the European experiments were performed on a Polish, Jewish, Russian and in part even a Gypsy public, the American researches were conducted using Japanese and hence yellow-skinned, raw material.[5]

Two other works having a bearing on the theme of medical experimentation on humans deserve mention. "Morton — a glimpse from medical history," a long essay on Morton, Jackson and Wells, the three co-discoverers of anaesthesia, contains a brief digression on the contributions to practical

---

5. Bjørneboe, *Moment of Freedom*, trans. by Esther Greenleaf Mürer (Chester Springs, PA: Dufour, 1999), 202. References to the other volumes of the "History of Bestiality" trilogy, *Powderhouse* and *The Silence*, are also to Mürer's translations (Dufour, 2000).

surgery by executioners and torturers from the Middle Ages to
the mid-19th century.[6] And in *Powderhouse* (1969) the executioner Lacroix describes scientific investigations of consciousness in guillotine-severed heads, with results which led to a ban
on further research in some countries. (152-156)

It must be stressed that Bjørneboe is by no means opposed
to scientific experimentation per se. His world view is a
thoroughly empirical one. He considers literature "an empirical
science"; his own writings a series of experiments — essays in
the sense of "attempt" or "trial." For him the idea of freedom
means first and foremost the freedom to experiment, to question:

> Nothing awakens such hate in secure, saved believers
> as skeptical, critical thought — as the desire to see for
> oneself, to test an inherited truth oneself before
> accepting it. For persons with this attitude "*nothing
> is sacred* "; no authority exists for them but the *true*
> authority which derives from greater insight, greater
> experience — from reality itself.[7]

For Bjørneboe freedom to experiment in the service of
truth cannot be divorced from compassion for the wretched,
the stranger, the deviant, the outsider. In *Semmelweis,* his epic
play about Ignaz Semmelweis's discovery of antisepsis and his
battle to win acceptance for his method, the protagonist not

6. Bjørneboe, "Morton — et glimt fra medisinens historie," *Samlede
Essays: Kultur II* (Oslo: Pax, 1996), 123-125.

7. Bjørneboe, "Anarchism — today?" (1971) trans. by Mürer, in
Degrees of Freedom: Anarchist Essays by and about Jens Bjørneboe
(Philadelphia: Protocol Press, 1998), 8. Original: "Anarkismen...
idag," *Samlede Essays: Politikk*: (Oslo: Pax, 1996), 213.

only challenges the status quo with his experiments, but dares to ask the medical authorities to risk their prestige for the benefit of people who are of "no account": prostitutes and other indigent or lower-class women. Semmelweis, like other medical healers in Bjørneboe's late work, is himself an outsider. Not only is he a foreigner — regarded by the Austrian medical establishment as "that crazy Hungarian" — but he takes seriously the ideas of such riffraff as whores and latrine cleaners, verifying them by his own experiments and using the results to challenge received "truths." Semmelweis battles the system and is personally destroyed by it, but his ideas prevail in the end.[8]

Bjørneboe sees the authority principle — what theologian Walter Wink calls "the domination system" — as a pervasive characteristic of society and a primary root of human evil; his target is the ways in which the struggle to gain or defend power takes precedence over healing truth.[9] *Semmelweis* and *Amputation* are two very different statements of his vision — the first historical, the other a futuristic fantasy in the prophetic dystopian tradition of Zamiatin, Huxley and Orwell.

---

8. Bjørneboe, *Semmelweis*, translated by Joe Martin (Los Angeles: Sun and Moon, 1998).

9. For an examination of Bjørneboe's views on authority with particular reference to the play *Semmelweis*, see Oddbjørn Johannessen, "The authoritarian and the 'traitors,'" trans. by Mürer on the website: < http://emurer.home.att.net/about/sem-oj.htm > The original: "Det autoritære og 'svikerne': et kortfattet studie med utgangspunkt i skuespillet *Semmelweis*," *Sørlandsk magasin* no. 7, 1991, 50-53.
Walter Wink discusses the domination system at length in *Engaging the Powers: Discernment and Resistance in a World of Domination* (Minneapolis: Fortress, 1992). For a briefer treatment, see his *The Powers that Be* (New York: Doubleday, 1998).

2.

Throughout his whole career, Jens Bjørneboe struggled continually to find forms which would embody the explosive kind of material he felt impelled to deal with, whether as novelist or as playwright. In *The Silence* (1973), the narrator pokes fun at his own lack of awareness of the theater's practicalities in a play he wrote as a young teenager (85f).

For purposes of comparison with *Amputation* it is instructive to refer back to the play version of *Ere the Cock Crows*, which had been refused by the Studio Theater with the comment: "Even though the theme may be current — timeless, in fact — the public runs away from such stuff." The novel presents formal difficulties of its own, owing largely to the undigested quality of the play version, which is perhaps too clearly visible in chapters 3-5 of the novel. But this visibility makes it possible to attempt a reconstruction of the original play, which is lost.

If my reconstruction is correct, the play's opening anticipates *Amputation* in its uncompromising brutality. Bjørneboe appears to have begun by presenting the horror of the research abstractly and impersonally; the rest of the play then probed the motivations and rationalizations of those responsible. The first act begins, I believe, with the camp's new commandant, Paul Heidebrand, orienting himself about the experiments by interviewing subordinates, plying them with alcohol to dull their sensibilties; while offstage we hear a prisoners' chorus being forced to rehearse a song to welcome a visiting SS-higher-up:

> HEIDEBRAND: Do you know if any of the vacci-
> nation records were *not* brought up to date?
> AIDE *(as if reading from a book)*: Jawohl, Standarten-
> führer! The transients are not included in the

statistics. But all the fever experiments are registered and entered in the records.

HEIDEBRAND (*suddenly alert*): What does "transient" mean?

AIDE: That is the designation for those who are inoculated with the disease just so they will have it. They aren't vaccinated first. Dr. Eger says that he keeps the bacteria cultures alive in them, so that one can just help oneself when infectious matter is needed.

HEIDEBRAND (*ponders. Gesturing toward the window*): Have *the ones out there* learned the song?

MAX: It took a couple hours, but now them's singin' just fine. (*Quickly leans forward to keep his balance.*)

HEIDEBRAND (*consults a paper. To AIDE*): Were there more doctors involved in the experiments besides those listed here?

AIDE: Jawohl, Standartenführer! A Danish doctor took part in the experiments, but he hasn't been here for a long time now.

HEIDEBRAND (*looks at his wristwatch. To MAX*): Obergruppenführer Dr. Scholz should arrive from Berlin before two o'clock. When he gets here we must have a little night-time roll call and welcome him with the song. We can let them sing it a couple times first. He'll appreciate it.

MAX clicks his heels, fighting to stay upright.

HEIDEBRAND: Were you present at all the experiments for the Air Force?

MAX (*trying to sound sober*): No.

AIDE (*coming to his rescue*): Not all of them, Standartenführer!

HEIDEBRAND: I don't mean every single experiment, but at all the different *types*.

MAX: I was only at the frost and pressure experiments. Not the others.

AIDE: You can be glad of that.

HEIDEBRAND (*to AIDE, after a pause*): Did *you*
attend all of them?

AIDE (*thinks about it, then counts on his fingers*):
Let's see: Air — one! The dry frost experiments
— two! The wet frost experiments — three!
Then we have the shipwreck experiments with
salt water — four! Then there were the ones
with distilled salt water! That's five. Chemical
salt water — six! The others — the ones with
mustard gas and the surgical experiments, they
were for the Army. But I've been at all the
types of experiments for the Air Force, yes.

HEIDEBRAND: Drink! Help yourselves! [10]

There are several more pages in this vein, steadily in-
creasing in intensity. If this was indeed how the play began,
the theater officials had a point: the audience would have run
retching from the hall in the first ten minutes. After the intense opening scene, however, the play gradually settles down
into a conventional drama in the Ibsen mold which then domi-
nated Norwegian theater almost exclusively.

---

10. Reconstructed from *Før Hanen Galer*, 67-69.

Bjørneboe was bitter about the rejection.[11] Nevertheless, it was probably a blessing. As things were to work out, Bjørneboe would not emerge as a dramatist until he had found a way to break free of Ibsen. In a 1963 essay on August Strindberg Bjorneboe writes:

> Ibsen's philosophical point of departure is handed-down moral ideas and conceptions about ideals — and he remains within these trains of thought all his life: The world is ordered, moral, logical. He does not wish it otherwise. In the same way his point of departure with respect to dramaturgical technique is also inherited and traditional... Ibsen does not want this otherwise than it is either. He perfects it and uses it. Ibsen completes and closes a period, a systematically ordered archive of a cosmos... The world order is an all-encompassing judicial archive. It is the bourgeois world which concludes with Ibsen.
>
> On a purely theatrical plane... Ibsen has become a burden, an immovable gravestone which preserves that form of theater which Ibsen mastered and therefore wished to keep unchanged. In dramatic world literature Strindberg has many descendants, Ibsen none. In his sterility too he was perfect.[12]

---

11. He wrote in the 1967 afterword: "Thus does one ensure that the Norwegian theater won't be plagued by authors writing for the stage.... Perhaps it's no great loss, but in any case it shows that the method — a brief and polite 'No thank you' — is effective insect powder against dramatic literature." (186)

12. Bjørneboe, "Strindberg, the fertile," trans. by Mürer. Original: "Strindberg — den fruktbare" (1963), *Samlede Essays: Teater* (Oslo: Pax, 1996), 27. < http://emurer.home.att.net/texts/strindberg.htm >

Bjørneboe's search for an alternative to Ibsen gained initial momentum from a long sojourn with the Berliner Ensemble, founded by Bertold Brecht, in 1959. During the next few years, until his stage debut in 1965, immersed himself in the work of Brecht and other non-Norwegian pioneers of modern theater.

The fullest statement of his emerging ideas on dramaturgy is his 1963 essay "The theater tomorrow," included in this volume. There and elsewhere he advocates a "psychosomatic" or "logos-somatic" theater which takes the form of a "high literary circus." As our thought-world becomes ever more abstract — with ever more horrendous physical effects, epitomized by Hiroshima and Nagasaki — the theater and the acting style must become correspondingly more concrete and physical.

> That is: the thought — in the form of image, metaphor — must become wholly visible. The metaphor must be taken literally, shown directly — so that there arises an intellectual process, made visible in a clear and logical series of images — of physical (*not mental, and not social either!*) situations. A contemporary theater will thus be scientific and philosophical, and circuslike and physical, all at the same time. Everything must become *action*, and there will be a definitive end to the old statuary declamation of "poetic" or "profound" speeches...

The first, shorter version of *Amputation* is Bjørneboe's first *published* play, antedating his stage debut with *Many Happy*

Returns! the following year.[13]   This early version, entitled "The Amputation" (note the definite article) may be regarded as a test of how his developing ideas will work out in practice. It borders on farce in its surrealistic lunacy, focusing on the contest between the two competing surgeons, whom Joe Martin likens to "red clowns from Hell — or the Marx Brothers in the age of technology." [14]

At the time Bjørneboe despaired of finding a theater with an acting style sufficiently acrobatic and physical to perform it. He later found the right troupe in the Swedish arena theater Friteatern, whose director, Martha Vestin, approached him in the fall of 1969. Joe Martin reports on a 1986 interview with Vestin:

> The revolution in performance techniques in the sixties — with the convergence of the influences of Brecht and Artaud with that of Grotowsky — made the venture possible... The language itself is direct, clownishly rough hewn, often fierce or violent, and the characters are made to order for those skilled in playing caricature...
>
>   The acting ensemble at Friteatern was comprised of people willing to do voice and body training of the most disciplined sort. The group paid a visit to Oslo and improvised the material. "This got him going," reports Vestin. The actors wrote stories about their

---

13. In the 1950s Bjørneboe published two short plays written for his Steiner school pupils in the school magazine, of which he was editor. They are included with his pedagogical essays.

14. Joe Martin, *Keeper of the Protocols: The Works of Jens Bjørneboe in the Crosscurrents of Western Literature* (New York: Peter Lang, 1996), 124-125.

characters' pasts during the process. It was then that Bjørneboe introduced the sequence of flashbacks to contrast with the brutal here-and-now activity in the theatre... The style of the performance was "farce, in Moliere's style" according to Vestin. But stylization slowly gave way during the 1½ hours to a closer, more brutal imitation of reality. The giant horse syringes grew smaller, more real and vicious looking, until — in the scene where a needle is used to kill Forgetmegenot — a real hypodermic needle was inserted under the skin of a real actor's belly. To build toward this "clinical" reality, actors did training with a doctor and nurse team to get the details down-pat. The theatre was set up as an "operating theatre," which lent itself both to theatricality and verisimilitude. Vestin found it unnecessary to use "sounds" of limbs falling into buckets, as the visual impact was sufficiently horrific. Vestin: "In the kind of theatre I do, the audience is participating in the event. Violence is very dangerous because the audience thinks, 'Oh — that poor actor.' Then they pull out of the play." [15]

3.

Bjørneboe has often been criticized for his obsession with physical violence and cruelty. For example, one review of *Amputation* was entitled "Bloody Bjørneboe, or: how to prostitute progressive literature." To this critic, "*Amputation* is an exceedingly primitive play, written with little art, and with the intention of producing a violent and ghastly effect... Appeal,

---

15. *Ibid.*, 124-125, 175.

message, the raising of awareness — it all drowns in blood and brutality." [16]

Similarly, In 1967 the Danish critic Ole Storm had written that *Ere the Cock Crows* "in my opinion used the German concentration camp doctors' cynical experiments with the prisoners as an excuse for writing sensationally about perversion and sadism." Bjørneboe sued Storm for a libel, saying that Storm had impugned his motives for writing the book. Bjørneboe told the court:

> The thread through my whole authorship is "the problem of evil." After all, that's my theme — it isn't a theme I've chosen; it has been an absolute necessity, never a choice... What I've written has been what is called today "engaged writing". But it has never been a *willed* engagement; it would have been more pleasant to write about idylls, about flowers and harmless things, about the welfare state's small sorrows and irritations. I've never been able to do that, I have been an "engaged writer" against my will — my engagement I've never been able to escape, never run away from. [17]

---

16. Eiliv Eide in *Bergens Tidende*, 25 February 1971, quoted by Janet Garton, *Jens Bjørneboe: Prophet without Honor* (Westport, CT: Greenwood Publication Group, 1985), 84.

17. Bjørneboe, "Fra en litterær injurieproces" (1968), *Samlede Essays: Kultur I* (Oslo: Pax, 1996), 205-206. For a brief account of the case see Fredrik Wandrup, *Jens Bjørneboe, mannen — myten — kunsten* (Oslo: Gyldendal, 1984), 55. Wandrup records that "Storm was directed by the municipal court to pay Bjørneboe 4000 kroner in damages. He appealed the case to the supreme court. There the judgment was overturned by four to three votes."

To shed more light on Bjørneboe's basic situation and temperament, it may be helpful to look at his 1955 essay on the 19th-century Norwegian bohemian and anarchist Hans Jæger. There he distinguishes two types of people who belong to "the spiritually motivated segment of humanity" and don't feel at home in this world. He describes these types variously as "romantics" and "radicals," "monks" and "Knights of the Grail," "melancholic" and "choleric."

> The "neoromantics" and "modernists" opt out of a wholly impossible society, they break the thread and more or less retire to the countryside and write about how terrible they feel... The radical acts out of the same basic experience, but through an entirely different temperament; he chooses to cure his unhappiness by fixing the world, by changing it so that it will be able to make room for his and others' humanity. Basically one can then speak of a melancholic and a choleric reaction.
>
> The radical maintains his volitional relation to reality, and he has the potential to gain the whole world, but with considerable risk of injury to his soul. He loses the umbilical cord to the metaphysical realm which in fact once set him in motion, and all his deeds end up in meaningless fights and empty busyness. The melancholic keeps the umbilical link to the stars and the cosmos, but at the risk of his withdrawal from humanity's leading to another amputation which isn't much better; he has lost the blood supply from earthly reality and its problems, he has

lost the world as a field for moral experimentation.[18]

Bjørneboe's work as a whole indicates that he felt a strong pull in both directions. Throughout his career he struggled to maintain a connection with both the metaphysical realm and with earthly reality. That struggle is at the heart of his last four novels, the "History of Bestiality" trilogy and *The Sharks*.

Perhaps his emergence as a dramatist helped to maintain a balance. Broadly speaking, melancholy predominates in the novels, choler in the plays. In any case, *Amputation* is a "choleric" work. (Note, however, that it is the melancholic — significantly named Mr. Forgetmenot — who resists any kind of "normalization.")

In *Moment of Freedom* (1966), the Servant of Justice describes the depressing experience of writing a "protocol" similar to *Ere the Cock Crows*:

> I studied the Doctors' Trials and the medical documents during this time, and little by little I understood that the eclipse of the sun had come. The birds stopped singing, the grass turned gray where it wasn't bloody, and the rivers overflowed with excrement, rotting entrails and severed limbs, just as in the sewers under the social camps in Mozart's land.
>
> I continued now, with protocol after protocol; ... a demeaning, annihilating labor, and again the darkness oozed in over me, steadily stronger and more impenetrably thick and suffocating. (202f, 205)

---

18. Bjørneboe, "Hans Jæger" (1955), trans. Mürer, *Jens Bjørneboe in English*: < http://emurer.home.att.net/texts/jaeger.htm >. Original: *Samlede Essays: Kultur I*, 112-113.

Of a subsequent "protocol," an exposé of prison conditions, the Servant of Justice adds that it "had an extremely
depressing effect on me in the long run, especially because I was
now sure that this whole long and painful record would be
written down without producing any effect. All I could do was
to put everything in, word by word, line by line, page by
page." (206)

The reference here is to Bjørneboe's sustained assault on
the Norwegian prison system. It began with a a series of
articles published in 1959-60, which was met with absolute
silence on the part of the authorities.[19] In a 1967 essay
Bjørneboe likens the establishment to the Bøyg, an enormous,
invisible, serpentine monster of Norse mythology:

So far the great Bøyg always wins without a fight.
The Bøyg's method is a war of sheer endurance and
attrition. And in almost all cases a fight between
departmental authorities and a single person will end
with economic and physical exhaustion of the individual. The situation is very simple: what makes the
Bøyg's method so ingenious and watertight is the fact
that the public men have all the advantages on their
side: they have all the resources at their disposal,
they have free legal and professional assistance, they
have the sympathy of the courts and all the depart-
ments within the bureaucracy on their side, they can
mobilize the whole system to their own advantage, in
a world of camaraderie and in-group loyalty. In addition they have both time and the national treasury on
their side: they can defend themselves during office

19. For a detailed account of Bjørneboe's battle with the Norwegian
judicial system see Garton, *op cit.*, chap. 6, "The Assault on the
Establishment," 59-68.

hours, and they can use public means, the taxpayers' money, for their own defense. They don't even need to think about making a living while the battle is in progress: we pay them to sit in their seats and quite simply just to be there, they are paid to exist, while they telephone, organize and arrange the war of attrition. This is, was and always has been the bureaucrats' true bulwark...[20]

Bjørneboe felt called to engagement, but suffered severe, prolonged depressions as well as feelings of hopelessness. One way of coping was what the narrator of *Moment of Freedom* calls "Florentine laughter":

Why is it that cruelty calls forth laughter? Those who founded this culture, that of the Renaissance, were all men who laughed at atrocities. The whole of our new world, our modern culture, was born in Tuscany; the whole of precise, empirical art and the whole of exact science — it all comes from the stone cities of Tuscany. And the Tuscans were feared for their laughter... They were great observers, cool and detached — they taught the world to distinguish between arbitrariness and law. Aretino laughed himself to death when he met his sister in a brothel, he was one of the few people in world history who notoriously died laughing...

But this laughter is the reason why the Tuscans invented science and the clear Tuscan drawing in their cool paintings; laughter means distance. Conversely:

---

20. Jens Bjørneboe, "The Righteous and the Innocent" (1967), trans. Mürer, <http://emurer.home.att.net/texts/boyg.htm>. Original: "De rettferdige og de uskyldige." *Samlede Essays: Kultur I*, 63.

where laughter is absent, madness begins. Every time I've had a chance to observe an outbreak of psychosis or a first-rate clinical anxiety neurosis the signal has been given in the absence of humor — the moment one takes the world with complete seriousness one is potentially insane. The whole art of learning to live means holding fast to laughter; without laughter the world is a torture chamber, a dark place where dark things will happen to us, a horror show filled with bloody deeds of violence... (112f)

In "The Amputation" Professor Vivaldi is not from Minsk as in the later version, but from Bologna. Shortly after his entry he addresses the audience:

VIVALDI. Ladies and gentlemen! In my country-man Dante's masterpiece, *The Divine Comedy,* there are some often-translated lines dealing with melancholy, clinical depression — in which Dante — and this corresponds to the teaching of the Church — refers to a certain gruesome pool of mud in Inferno... for those who in the light of the sun have fallen into the vice of melancholy...

"We were despondent in the mild air which rejoices in the sun!" Today with the development of anarcho-surgery we have fortunately eliminated Dante's problem — namely by means of a surgical knife in the brain mantle or nervous system, at the anatomically exactly right place!

This passage is cut in the later version. In the meantime Bjørneboe had used the same quotation from Dante in the "Praiano Papers" section of *Moment of Freedom*, adding:

Can Dante possibly be unaware that with this slimy, muddy pool of blood and shit he is giving an exact description of the punishment for melancholy here and now? No, it isn't possible, he must have known that the very despondency, the melancholy or depression itself, is a *substance* — rotting, viscous, stinking matter mixed with blood, which one wades in up to one's knees. In the same way *time* is also a substance, viscous and heavy-flowing...

For no conscious person can live without this ability to laugh at cripples, disease and suffering. To laugh at maltreated animals and children, to laugh at everything. Without the Florentine laughter one goes mad... Without laughter you sit fast in the pool of excrement, and you will slowly go into decomposition, into autolysis, you will fall apart, and yourself turn into living excrement...

All the great masters from Tuscany's ateliers took their sketchbooks along when they went to watch the public executions. (120f)

Florentine laughter is noticeably absent in *Ere the Cock Crows*. In *Amputation* it dominates, perhaps spinning out of control.

JENS BJØRNEBOE: CHRONOLOGY

1920 Born October 9 in Kristiansand, Norway.

1935 Takes year off from school because of illness. "I read real books instead."

1936 Works as cabin boy over the Atlantic on one of his father's ships.

1938 Expelled from Kristiansand Cathedral School.

1939 Expelled from the high school in Flekkefjord. Travels to central Europe.

1940 Gets his *artium* (high-school diploma) as a private student in Drammen. Travels to Spitzbergen as a seaman. Begins study at the State school of Arts and Crafts. After it is closed he continues to study art at the painter Axel Revold's illegal art academy.

1943 Notified the the Germans are about to conscript him for forced labor; flees to Sweden.

1943-45 Studies painting at the Royal Academy of Art and under the painter Isaac Grünewald in Stockholm.

1945 Returns to Norway. Marries Lisel Funk.

1946 Oil painting at the fall exhibition in Oslo. Exhibit of 45 paintings in Kristiansand.

1950 Begins teaching carpentry at the Steiner School. Later becomes full-time teacher at the school in all subjects.

1951 *Dikt* [Poems].

1952 *Før Hanen Galer* [Ere the Cock Crows], novel.

1953 *Ariadne*, poems.

1955 *Jonas*, novel.

1957 Leaves the Steiner School after breakup of marriage and resurgence of drinking problem. *Under en Hårdere Himmel* [Under a Sterner Heaven], novel.

1957-59 Travels around Italy and Central Europe.

1958   *Vinter i Bellapalma* [Winter in Bellapalma],novel; *Den Store By* [The Great City], poems.

1959   *Blåmann* [Little Boy Blue], novel. Serves a jail sentence for drunk driving.

1959-60 Series of newspaper articles criticizing the Norwegian prison system.

1960   *Den Onde Hyrde* [The Evil Shepherd], novel.

1961   First marriage dissolved. Marries Tone Tveteraas.

1964   *Drømmen og Hjulet* [The Dream and the Wheel], novel.

1965   *Til Lykke med Dagen* [Many Happy Returns], musical play.

1966   *Frihetens Øyeblikk* [Moment of Freedom], experimental novel; first volume of the trilogy popularly known as *The History of Bestiality*. *Uten en Tråd* [Without a Stitch], pornographic novel, confiscated.
Fugleelskerne [The Bird-Lovers], musical play.

1967   The case of *Without a Stitch* comes to trial; book banned.

1968   *Without a Stitch II* published in Denmark. Dedicated to the Norwegian Supreme Court. *Aske, Vind og Jord* [Ashes, Wind and Earth], selected poems. *Norge, mitt Norge* [Norway, my Norway], essays.

1969   *Semmelweis*, play; *Kruttårnet* [Powderhouse], second volume of the *The History of Bestiality* trilogy.

1970   *Vi som Elsket Amerika* [We Who Loved America], essays; *Amputasjon* [Amputation], play.

1972   *Hertug Hans* [Duke Hans], historical novella written in 1948. *Politi og Anarki* [Police and Anarchy], essays.

1973   *Stillheten* [The Silence], third volume of trilogy; *Tilfellet Torgersen* [The Torgersen Case], play.

1974   *Haiene* [The Sharks], novel.

1975   Moves to the island of Veierland near Tønsberg.

1976   *Dongery* [Blue Jeans], musical play; *Våpenløs* [Weaponless] (recording, reading own poetry). Found dead May 10.

Posthumous publications:

1976 *Under en Mykere Himmel* [Under a Gentler Sky],essays.
  Rød Emma [Red Emma], unfinished play. Pirate edition
  stopped by family.
1977 *Om Brecht* [On Brecht], essays. *Samlede Dikt* [Collected
  Poems]. *Lanterner* [Lanterns], short pieces and epistles.
1978 *Om Teater* [On Theater], essays.
1979 *Bøker og Mennesker* [Books and People], reviews and
  articles.
1995-96 Collected Works issued in hardcover, 21 volumes.

Adapted from Fredrik Wandrup, *Jens Bjørneboe: Mannen,
Myten, Kunsten* (Oslo: Gyldendal Norsk Forlag, 1984).

JENS BJØRNEBOE: OTHER WORKS IN ENGLISH

PLAYS

The Bird Lovers, translated by Frederick Wasser (Los Angeles: Sun & Moon, 1994).
Semmelweis, translated by Joe Martin (Los Angeles: Sun & Moon, 1998).

NOVELS

The Least of These [= *Jonas*], translated by Bernt Jebsen & Douglas K. Stafford (Indianapolis: Bobbs-Merill, 1959).
Without A Stitch, translated by Walter Barthold (New York: Grove, 1969).
The Sharks, translated by Esther Greenleaf Mürer (Norwich, England: Norvik, 1992).
"History of Bestiality" Trilogy, translated by Esther Greenleaf Mürer (Chester Springs, PA: Dufour):

(1) *Moment of Freedom* (1999);
(2) *Powderhouse* (2000);
(3) *The Silence* (2000).

ESSAYS

Degrees of Freedom: Essays on Anarchism, translated by Esther Greenleaf Mürer (Philadelphia: Protocol, 1998).

WEBSITE

< http://emurer.home.att.net >

ABOUT JENS BJØRNEBOE

Janet Garton, *Jens Bjørneboe: Prophet Without Honor* (Westport & London: Greenwood, 1985).

Joe Martin, *Keeper of the Protocols: The Works of Jens Bjørneboe in the Crosscurrents of Western Literature* (New York: Peter Lang, 1996).

SOURCES

"The Theater Tomorrow" — "Teatret i morgen," *Ordet*, 1963. Collected in Jens Bjørneboe, *Om Teater: Samlede Essays* (Oslo: Pax Forlag, 1978, 1996), 133-147.

The Amputation — "Amputasjonen: manasjespill i én akt," *Ordet*, 1964. Collected in *Om Teater* (Oslo: Pax, 1978), 59-85.

Work on a new version — From *Om Teater* (Oslo: Gyldendals Norsk Forlag, 1978).

Amputation — *Amputasjon* (Oslo: Gyldendal, 1970); collected in *Samlede Skuespill* (Oslo: Pax, 1973, 1995).

JB letter & programme — Solrun Hoaas, personal collection.

Katharine Brisbane, "Amputation," *Theatre Australia*, 34, July 1977.

Oddbjørn Johannessen, "Jens Bjørneboe and the Norwegian Theater" — "Jens Bjørneboe og norsk teater," *Sørlandsk magasin* No. 12, 1996, 17-19. Update April 2001 for the current volume.

Esther Greenleaf Mürer, "Mad Scientists and Moral Outrage: The Genesis of Jens Bjørneboe's *Amputation*" — first publication.

SOLRUN HOAAS was born in Norway in 1943, but spent fourteen early years in China and Japan. At Oslo University she earned a degree in Arts and Social Anthropology and was active in student theater. In Japan, she studied theater in Kyoto on a post-graduate scholarship. In 1972, she settled in Canberra, Australia, taught secondary French and then worked as a research assistant and tutor in the Japanese Department at the Australian National University while completing a Masters Degree in Asian Studies. In this period she directed one-act plays, translated from Norwegian and Japanese, and wrote non-fiction. In 1975, together with her then husband Roger Pulvers, she visited Jens Bjørneboe in Oslo. Two years later Pulvers directed *Amputation* in her translation. At the same time she began filming in Okinawa and earned a graduate diploma in film in Melbourne. Since then she has written, produced and directed a number of Japan-related films, including the award-winning documentaries *Sacred Vandals* (1983) and *Green Tea and Cherry Ripe* (1989), the feature film *Aya* (1990) and two documentaries from Korea, *Pyongyang Diaries* (1997) and *Rushing to Sunshine* (2001). She lives in Melbourne.

ESTHER GREENLEAF MÜRER, born in 1935, was inspired by the reading of Jens Bjorneboe's novel *Powderhouse* to begin the monumental project of translating the entire "History of Bestiality" trilogy: *Moment of Freedom*, *Powderhouse* and *The Silence*. The project was completed at the end of the millennium, and all three novels were published by Dufour Editions. Mürer has also translated Bjørneboe's novel *The Sharks* (Norvik Press). Her website, Jens Bjørneboe in English < http://emurer.home.att.net/ >, features translations of smaller works — poems and essays — as well as bibliographies and critical articles about him from many sources. She also hosts a website, Quakers and the Arts Historical Sourcebook: < http://home.att.net/ ~ quakart >

Other Xenos Translations

Edvard Hoem, *Ave Eva: A Norwegian Tragedy*, translated from the Nynorsk ("New Norwegian") by Frankie Belle Shackelford. A brooding novel from the North, part romance, part murder mystery, part social commentary, mixed together in an intense spiritual quest. ISBN 1-879378-42-6.

Emil Draitser, *The Supervisor of the Sea & other stories*, translated from the Russian. Soviet Russia, émigré America and the fantastic beyond. "Draitser's humor is so deeply philosophical that the reader doesn't notice at times where the comedy ends and the tragedy begins." *(World Literature Today)* ISBN 1-879378-47-7.

Lutz Rathenow, *The Fantastic Ordinary World of Lutz Rathenow: Poems, Plays & Stories*, translated from the German by Boria Sax & Imogen von Tannenberg. Satires, skits and grotesqueries conveying the maddening humdrumness of the ultimate police state. Bilingual. ISBN 1-879378-31-0.

Alfredo de Palchi, *The Scorpion's Dark Dance*, translated from the Italian by Sonia Raiziss. Stark poems written by a young man in an Italian prison after World War II. Bilingual. ISBN 1-879378-05-1.

Antonio Porta, *Dreams & Other Infidelities*, translated from the Italian by Anthony Molino. Stories halfway between dream and waking that explore the uncensored territory of the mind, by a renowned experimentalist. ISBN 1-879378-37-X.

Manlio Santanelli, *Emergency Exit*, translated from the Italian by Anthony Molino with Jane House. A ferocious and funny play set in an earthquake zone. "Extraordinary, intended for audiences who hunger for the rare and beautiful." (Eugene Ionesco) ISBN 1-879378-40-X.

All titles in paperback

Available at www.xenosbooks.com or 909.370.2229
Also from Small Press Distribution (www.spdbooks.org)
or Amazon (www.amazon.com).